THE WARLOCK LORD

RITE WORLD: RITE OF THE WARLOCK

JULIANA HAYGERT

AUTHOR'S NOTE

I HOPE YOU ENJOY READING *THE WARLOCK LORD*!

DON'T FORGET TO SIGN UP FOR MY NEWSLETTER TO FIND OUT about new releases, cover reveals, giveaways, and more!

IF YOU WANT TO SEE EXCLUSIVE TEASERS, HELP ME DECIDE ON covers, read excerpts, talk about books, etc, join my reader group on Facebook: Juliana's Club!

RITE WORLD

Welcome to the RITE WORLD!

RITE WORLD is what I call a super series title, where a few of my series will take place. This means the world is the same for each of these series, and you'll see several of the same characters here and there.

Right now, I have two series in this world:

Rite of the Vampire
and
Rite of the Warlock

Coming later in 2019:
Rite of the Wolf

Welcome to the RITE WORLD! I hope you have fun here!

1

LUANA

From behind the bushes, I spied the herd of deer in a little valley. There were at least a dozen of them, eating the overgrown greens and warming themselves in the last rays of sunlight.

Clueless of the werewolf pack surrounding them.

Everyone ready? I sent my thoughts to the wolves who had volunteered to come with me. When in wolf form, our minds were linked and we communicated via thought. The alpha was able to control this connection, sending thoughts to each wolf or blocking them. However, as the youngest and the first female alpha of our pack in more than two centuries, I was still trying to learn my newfound powers.

And a bunch of other things.

Like controlling a large pack of aggressive werewolves.

Ready. Wyatt was the first to respond, as usual.

But nobody else did.

I swallowed a growl, lest the deer hear me. I could see the

other wolves across the valley. Moon be damned, why didn't they answer me?

Are you ready? I tried again.

A handful of half-assed yeses sounded in my mind.

After we killed this herd and dragged them back to our pack for this damned feast tonight, I would have a talk with these wolves. I was their goddamn alpha. They had to do better than this.

Set, I told the wolves. The ears of one deer perked up. *Now!*

Teeth bared, I jumped from behind the bushes and—

Wait.

Startled by the command in Charles's voice, I skid to a stop right in front of the herd. I glanced around, realizing only Wyatt and I had attacked, and now the herd fled from us.

What are you waiting for? I put as much bite as I could into my words. A few wolves stepped forward, but they were too slow for my taste.

Instead of catching the entire herd in one fell swoop, we only got five deer before the others escaped.

When it was clear that was all we were going to get, I turned around and bared my teeth at Charles. *What the hell was that?*

Charles strutted out from behind the bushes. He stared me down with his dark brown eyes. Even though he was at least twice my size—maybe more in our wolf forms—I stood my ground. I wouldn't buck to this big bully.

I'm sorry. I just thought it wasn't the right time to attack. His voice dripped with sarcasm.

I let out a low growl. *Did you forget who I am?*

Charles growled in response. *Believe me, I have not.*

Then you know you have to obey me. Everyone does.
Unfortunately.

I couldn't believe he was being this direct. This stupid. And right in front of a bunch of wolves, who now surrounded us. I puffed my chest. *I don't care if you think it's fair or not. It is what it is. And you obey me until it changes.*

How about we change it now?

It was all the warning I got before he jumped on me. I barely had time to move back and avoid his hit and his sharp teeth.

What the hell? I directed to his mind only, but Charles didn't answer me. He was too busy circling me, preparing for another attack. *Charles, stop this now.*

Again, he didn't answer me. Instead, like a bulldozer, Charles ran toward me. I jumped to the side, but not before his paw found purchase on my side. His nails sank into my skin.

I let out a howl as the pain registered.

Shocked. I was shocked. In my year as alpha, I had heard rumors and insults, I had been glared at, but I had never been challenged like this. And I was certain Charles wasn't fooling around.

This was a challenge.

A challenge to become alpha.

Which meant, Charles would only stop once he killed me. Damn it.

In my stupor, I barely resisted when Charles careened into me. I slammed against the hard ground, and he stepped over me, his sharp teeth close to my neck.

Give up, Luana, he said in my thoughts. *Let me win this fight and I won't kill you. Let me become the alpha then become my mate. We can rule the pack together.*

The rumors had been right. Charles didn't only want to take the mantle of the alpha from me, but he also wanted me as a mate. As if he could decide that. We had stood side by side several times, and the mating bond hadn't snapped into place. I wasn't his mate and he knew it.

It didn't matter, because I would never be his mate, bond or no bond. Charles was a conceited and selfish wolf, who was even worse in human form. And not that handsome.

Finding strength in the depths of my core, I swiped a paw sideways, making Charles lose his footing. I pushed against him and rose to my feet.

I snarled at him. *Never.*

He showed me his sharp teeth. *Such a loss.*

Then he attacked again.

I sidestepped him, trying to think this through. As the alpha, I had become stronger and faster, but Charles was probably still stronger, not to mention a bigger and a more experienced fighter. If I wanted to win this fight, I would have to be fast.

Charles turned around and came at me again. He snapped his teeth close to my hind leg, and I jumped forward, putting distance between us.

Stop running from me, Charles said in my head.

Letting him think I was obeying him, I stood my ground. Charles snarled and charged me again. I waited—until the last second. Then I sidestepped him, angling my body. I jumped over him. Off balance, he hit the ground. I pressed my paw down on his snout and snapped my teeth an inch from his throat.

I'm not going to kill you. His eyes widened in surprise. *I won't be that kind of alpha. But be warned. Next time you challenge me, I'll make an example out of you.*

I stepped back and held my ground, afraid Charles would attack me again. To my surprise, he pushed up to his wobbly legs, his head low.

You'll regret this, he whispered in my mind.

And I believed him.

I DIDN'T REGRET TAKING DOWN ULRIC. HE HAD BEEN AN EVIL alpha with only his pride and power in mind. He had sent me, a young, lower-ranked wolf, on what was supposed to be an easy mission, but looking back, I was sure he thought I wouldn't survive. He had probably expected me to die when he sent me to spy on the vampires of DuMoir Castle. He never imagined I would have been captured and turned into a blood slave.

My stomach turned. I hated remembering those days, but things got better when I allied with Drake, who was now lord of DuMoir Castle. For a vampire, Drake was a decent man and wanted peace between the vampires and the other races. Because he had helped me and given me a family when my pack had abandoned me, I trusted him wholeheartedly. He and his mate, Thea, the Witch Queen of the Silverblood coven.

No, I didn't regret killing Ulric, but I did regret becoming the alpha. At first, it had been part of the plan— as alpha, the wolves of the Dark Vale pack would have to obey me during the battle when Drake and Thea retook DuMoir Castle. It had worked, but I wished there had been another way. Maybe if another wolf had been by my side, I could have let him take down Ulric and become the alpha. Then, I could have been his beta and avoided all the hateful glares—the same ones I felt now as I walked out of my cabin.

Since my fight with Charles, we had dragged the handful of deer back to our village, then I disappeared inside my cabin, while the others took care of the feast's preparations.

Back in human form, I washed the deer's blood and the dirt from the hard ground from my body, scrubbing the sponge over my skin, as if I could scour away more than dirt. Maybe my fate too?

After the shower, I donned leather pants and a suede vest and brushed my long hair down my back. Then, after a hundred deep breaths, I left the safety of my cabin and faced the wolves outside.

The pinprick of everyone's hateful glares sent goose bumps down my spine, but I did my best to stay calm, to control my heartbeat and my breathing, so they couldn't hear just how much I detested all of this—and use it to destroy me.

As much as I hated being alpha, I hated the idea of being killed even more.

I hadn't even taken five steps before Wyatt showed up in front of me, holding a glass of our artisan beer.

"I thought you might want something to drink," he said, smiling at me.

I eyed the glass. If it were Charles or any other werewolf, I would think the drink might be poison, but Wyatt was different. He was a teenager, who had lost his parents as a child, and because of that, the pack had raised him. He had had little guidance, but he was a loyal wolf nonetheless. I remembered him from before my mission, and he had always struck me as an upbeat and optimistic kid. Now a young man, he hadn't changed much.

And he seemed to like me as his alpha.

At least one wolf in the pack did.

I took the glass from him. "Thank you."

He stepped to my side and gestured down the road. "It's almost ready."

I looked around. Since werewolves decided to become more human than wolf many centuries ago, our pack had adopted an old human village with a handful of dirt packed roads and frail wooden houses lining them. With time, the wolves paved the roads with limestones and reinforced and expanded the houses. Despite the many wells for water and generators for electricity, the village still had a pre-Industrial feel to it.

My house was close to the edge of the forest and about eight houses from the center of the village, where a square was located. Following Wyatt's gesture, we walked toward the square.

If the weight of the stares from the people walking by my house and coming to the feast had been heavy before, it was nothing compared to the moment I stepped into the square and joined the rest of the wolves.

After the DuMoir battle, our numbers dwindled, but we still had about a hundred wolves in our pack—which was a record since wolves didn't do well in larger groups.

And right now, all the wolves stared at me and silence filled the air.

I cleared my throat. "Enjoy the feast, everyone." I waved toward the tables set to one side of the square, where the food and drink were spread out.

Slowly, the wolves resumed chatting and laughing. Slowly, everyone ignored me. Slowly, I let out a long breath.

My relief was short-lived as I approached the big bonfire

in the center of the square. Logs surrounded the fire, serving as benches, and on two of those logs sat Charles and his band of hateful wolves.

He stared at me, his dark eyes gleaming with the flicker of the fire. He raised his mug of beer toward me, then tipped it back, finishing it in two big gulps. The rest of his group patted his back and yelled, like drunks in a bar.

I shuddered, feeling like a stranger in my pack.

"Luana, my dear pup." I cringed at Patricia's voice. She was an elder she-wolf, who thought she was some kind of counselor to the alphas. She was probably the oldest wolf here, over a hundred years old, though she didn't look a day older than fifty. The old woman stepped in front of me, looking more like a Romani in her long dress and bangles than a werewolf, and she smiled wide, showing off her yellowed teeth. "There you are." She gestured to the table, where the limbs of the deer were now displayed—most of them still dripping with blood. "Thank you for securing our feast."

Was she being sarcastic? I could never tell with her. She was the kind of person who smiled even when she was handing out an insult.

"You're welcome," I said, unsure what she really wanted. Because I knew she wanted something. She never started a conversation without a clear purpose.

She hooked her frail arm on mine and tugged me forward. I let the old woman guide me through the crowd in the square, because I wanted to hear what she had to say. Probably more gossip and her own reasoning about it. I was so sick and tired of gossip and rumors.

And an unruly pack that looked down on its alpha.

"I heard Charles gave you a hard time," she said in a low

voice. With our enhanced senses, I was sure half the pack heard her. "He can be such a prick sometimes."

I steered us to the edge of the square, where it met one of the roads, and turned to her. "What do you want?"

She widened her eyes, pretending to be shocked by my tone. "My dear pup, I only want what's best for the pack."

I cringed again. I hated when she called me 'dear pup.' One, I wasn't a pup, and two, I wasn't dear to her. Not really. "And what would that be?"

She puffed her chest, preparing for a speech. "I believe we can't live as we used to. Werewolf packs have always been patriarchal, where females weren't allowed to move up the ranks. Unfortunately, the few female alphas we've had before didn't last." Her tone was calm and clear, and I frowned. The two females who had reached the alpha status in our pack had gotten there because they had been mates of the alphas when they died of natural causes. They assumed the position for a brief time—until a male wolf challenged their position and took over the alpha mantle. "But times are changing. I think we finally have one that will change history."

Still feeling on the defensive, I crossed my arms. Was she really saying what I thought she was saying? "You think I can hold my position?"

"I do, but you might need help."

And here we went. "And who would help me?"

"A mate."

I blinked at her, sure I had heard her wrong. Wasn't she just praising the future and the end of male dominance? "What?"

"Think about, my dear pup. As females, we're naturally weaker than males. A female alpha doesn't have much of a future, unless she has a strong male as her mate. He'll help her secure her place. Especially if she bears pups who will strengthen the line of succession."

I stared at her in horror. She was really telling me to get a mate and procreate. Just like that. "I don't need a male by my side. I can steer this ship alone."

She tilted her head, her eyes narrowing. "Do you really believe that? Didn't Charles just challenge you? Tomorrow, it'll be a stronger wolf, and eventually, you'll succumb."

My brows curled down at the thought. I wasn't afraid of losing the alpha position, but I didn't want to be hurt, or killed, in the process. However, what really made me sick was that most wolves in the pack still thought Ulric had been an amazing alpha. He had been ruthless and cold and greedy. He had brought more comfort and riches to the pack—at the cost of others. No, I didn't like that. On this matter, I agreed with Drake and Thea. All races could live together in peace. We just needed respect and courtesy.

If I succumbed, if I were killed and another wolf secured my position, then our pack was doomed, and peace with the vampires and the witches would be gone.

I couldn't let that happen.

I clenched my fists until I felt my nails digging into my palms. "And I bet you have someone in mind."

She nodded. "Charles."

What? I picked at my ears, once again sure I couldn't have heard her right. "I'm sorry. I thought you mentioned the wolf who just tried to kill me."

"I did," Patricia said, seriously. "He's not the strongest wolf in the pack, but he's strong enough. And half of this pack is under his thumb. If you mated with him, then they would all be under your thumb."

Even if the idea of having Charles as my partner didn't

disgust me, there was another problem to consider. "You do realize the mating bond isn't something that can be forced, right?"

Besides, Charles, or any other wolf in this pack, would use me as a pawn. I would hold the title, but I bet that as soon as I mated with one of them, they would steal my power. They would rule instead of me.

"Then find another one," she said, her voice gaining a slight hard edge. "Search for your precious mating bond among our pack, but do it fast. Otherwise, you're doomed."

She spun on her heels and marched back to the crowd. I watched as she joined a group of she-wolves near the bonfire and started talking animatedly. Patricia's mate had been killed a long time ago, and her only son had mated with a wolf from another pack—a rare event—and moved to his mate's pack. Patricia was alone here.

It seemed she was now trying to make an ally out of me. What was her real intention?

To her right, three werewolves brought out Spanish guitars and other instruments. In no time, there was music mixed with the chatter and the laughter around the square. There was plenty of food and drink.

Every wolf in the pack seemed happy. Carefree.

It was a shame I wasn't.

I WENT BACK TO WHERE IT ALL STARTED.

The freaking Silverblood estate. This place, with its expansive gardens and sprawling mansion, was home.

At least that was what Thea had said when we moved here after the battle of DuMoir Castle, over a year ago. I didn't have the heart to tell her this cursed place had never been my home and never would be. There were too many bad memories etched in each of these walls; I couldn't forget them.

But there were moments when Thea and Aurora weren't being witches, or the Witch Queen and the Queen of All Witches, but a loving mother and a happy daughter, that I could almost endure this place.

Like now.

I sat under the shade of a tree while Thea stood a few feet away under the mid-afternoon sun. Aurora ran around her mother, wobbling with each step and giggling each time she tripped.

The little girl, with her black curls and sea-green eyes, was pure joy—and magic. At only a few weeks after her first birthday, she could barely speak, but she could perform amazing magic.

Still running, she joined her palms and white sparks crackled from her hands. Several little blue chicks appeared around her. She let out a loud laugh.

Until she stepped on one of the chicks by mistake and the little thing exploded in blue glitter.

Aurora stopped moving, her lower lip pouted, and big, fat tears filled her eyes.

"Oh, sweetie." Thea knelt and opened her arms. The little girl fell into her mother's warm embrace. "It's okay, honey. They are just magic, remember? We can make more."

Thea waved her hand, and soon there were not only chicks, but also baby ducks and turtles and bunnies swarming the garden. Aurora's tears disappeared, and she commenced running around the magical figures.

Exhaling a sigh, Thea sat down beside me. "She tires me."

"But you're happy about it," I said.

She looked me as if I was crazy. "Of course. I love that she tires me." Her blue eyes returned to the child, and something that I could only label as joy glowed from her entire expression.

Now jumping over the magical ducks and chicks and bunnies, Aurora giggled each time one exploded in colorful sparkles, then she conjured more.

"Her magic is impressive."

Thea glanced at me. "So is yours."

I sighed. Yes and no. Because I had been raised as a human slave, I hadn't known I was a warlock, a male witch, until recently. Morda, the previous ruler of the Silverblood coven, had threatened to kill me and my powers awoke. I had used them to save myself. But I was a twenty-four-year-old warlock with no prior magic experience. By some freaking miracle, I had been able to help during the DuMoir battle and kill Soraya, one of my worst oppressors.

Since then, Thea had been teaching me magic. I wasn't the worst student, but I knew I still had a long way to go before I was in control of my powers.

"I guess," I muttered, conflicted.

Thea elbowed my arm. "What is it?"

I forced a small smile for her sake. "Nothing. I'm fine."

She narrowed her eyes. I was sure she was going to launch into an endless speech about how she was my friend who wanted to help me and that she would find a way to fix whatever was wrong—not that I doubted her. I truly believed she had my best interest at heart, but there were things that not even the great Thea, or the great Drake for that matter, could fix.

And one of them was the cursed hole in my soul.

But, before Thea could say anything, Aurora threw herself at me. I hustled to catch her before she hit her head on the ground and embraced the silly girl.

"Kee-lam," she called in her sweet voice. She slipped her soft little hand into mine and tugged. "Pay."

Play. She always wanted to play.

"Keeran and mommy are talking now," Thea said.

Aurora turned to Thea and pouted. "Pay."

"It's okay," I whispered, unable to resist those huge, pretty eyes and that pout. "Help me up." She tugged on my hand again, and I pretended she was actually pulling me. I groaned. "Just a little more."

I jumped up and she giggled.

This, right here, was good. It was nice. I had a place to live, food to eat, a couple of friends who cared about me. There was a sweet little girl who loved playing with me. Thanks to Drake and Thea, we were now living in an era of peace, where there were no blood slaves, and witches, vampires, and werewolves weren't at war. We still hadn't heard one word from the fae, but that was okay as long as they stayed in their realm. I had everything a person could ask for, but I still felt like something was missing. Like I didn't belong here.

I spied over my shoulder, to the half dozen witches standing near the back porch of the mansion, whispering among themselves. Their eyes were on me, and I knew what they were saying.

It was hard to ignore them since they were everywhere inside this cursed mansion.

Aurora bumped into me, and I snapped my attention back to her. She giggled as she stepped over a pink bunny and tripped on her own feet. Forgetting about those cursed witches, I caught Aurora, firmly gripping her torso from under her arms and spun her around. Her laughter echoed through the garden. The colorful animals jumped up and down, as if following the beat of her laughter.

I set her down carefully so she wouldn't be dizzy and fall again. The animals crowded around us. Using her powers, Aurora conjured yellow birds and brown snails and purple butterflies and pink kittens. She danced around them, as happy as any one-year-old girl should be.

I wished her life free from evil witches, hungry werewolves or greedy vampires. I wished only good and beautiful things for her. I wished for her to become the good in our world, and for her to rule with a kind, joyful heart.

Remembering what I had once seen on TV when I was a kid, I channeled my magic and cast a small marble of power. I threw it at the ground. It cracked with a loud pop, and colorful sparkles jumped out of them. Humans had called them bang snaps—mine was just an improved version filled with magic.

Aurora's eyes rounded, and her little mouth made a big O. Then, she clapped and giggled, shouting, "'Gain, 'gain."

I opened my hand and a dozen magical marbles appeared in my palm. I handed a few to her and threw the rest myself.

Thea stood and smiled at me. "That's great control of your magic, if you haven't noticed."

I fought the urge to roll my eyes at her. Truth be told, I liked playing with this little girl. Who knew I would like kids so much? Or perhaps it was just Aurora. She was special. One of a kind.

"'Gain, 'gain!" Aurora cried.

I conjured more. When those were gone, Aurora cast more—bigger marbles this time.

To keep playing with her, I cast more, but just as I was about to throw a couple on the ground, I noticed the grass around us crackling with power. The green blades had absorbed some of the magic.

Aurora threw a handful of marbles a couple of feet away.

It hit the ground with a loud boom and magic exploded in a colorful wave.

With the force of the explosion, Aurora was pushed back, right into me. I hugged her to my chest, shielding her as the heat and power of the wave washed over my back. It crackled and burned, a slight heat that made me twist my back, but hopefully hadn't done any real damage.

Aurora whimpered in my arms. I looked down at her. "Are

you okay?" I turned her around and took a good look at her. She seemed scared, but otherwise fine.

I heard another whimper and my breath caught. "Thea," I whispered, realizing she had been the closest to the impact area.

With Aurora in my arms, I stood. Colorful smoke covered the area around us. "Thea!"

"Right here." She coughed. The smoke dissipated a little, and I was able to see Thea several feet away from where Aurora threw the marbles—in Drake's arms.

The smoke faded a little more, taking any residual energy away with it.

Slowly, Drake put Thea down. Aurora jerked in my arms and I let her go. She ran to her parents, who embraced her tight.

"H-how did you get here so fast?" I asked, relieved. Drake had been in one of the mansion's libraries, studying some important files.

"I needed a break. I was on my way here, already outside the mansion, when I felt the power crackling and heard the explosion." He had used his super speed to run to Thea and take her out of the blast range. Better safe than sorry. "What happened?"

"I-I ..."

"Aurora and Keeran were playing," Thea started. "She threw—"

"It was the warlock!" I turned to the new voice and flinched at the sight of the witches who had been watching from the porch marching toward us, their vicious eyes set on me. Alma, the ringleader, halted a few feet away and pointed her finger at me. "The warlock hurt Thea!"

"No, he didn't!" Thea retorted, her eyes narrowing.

"What do you call that, then?" Dinah asked. She was right at the top with Alma when it came to leading my fan club. "The warlock deliberately made little bombs charged with magic and threw them at your feet! He was practically attacking you, my queen."

Thea shook her head. "That's nonsense."

"It's not, my queen," Alma said. "We've been warning you since you first insisted in taking this abomination in." Abomination? I understood they weren't particularly welcoming of my kind, but abomination? I clenched my fists tight. These freaking witches were getting on my nerves. "He is a threat. Not only to you and us, but to the entire witch community. Having a warlock will destabilize our peace."

"We won't let that happen," Drake said, his voice firm. "Just like when we intervene and saved the world from Morda and Alex, we'll do it again."

Dinah jerked her finger at me again. "Then start by getting rid of *that*. He's the real threat here."

"He should be banished," a witch suggested.

"Or killed!" another one said.

"That's enough." Thea passed Aurora to Drake and stepped forward, her blue eyes murderous. "Keeran is my guest and an important part of our society. Consider him an honorary member of the Silverblood coven. You better treat him with respect, before I take severe actions against anyone who goes against my wishes. Understood?"

Alma huffed. Dinah took a step back. The rest of their troupe either lowered their heads or looked anywhere but at Thea and me.

"We'll talk more about this later," Alma said before spinning around and marching away.

Her troupe scurried after her.

As soon as they were out of hearing distance, Thea turned to me, her eyes soft. "Don't let their words affect you."

"Easier said than done."

She approached me. "Keeran ... what happened here was an accident. You were playing with Aurora and things got a little out of hand. I believe that even if Drake hadn't moved me out of the way, I wouldn't have been hurt. I don't think there was enough magic in that explosion to hurt me."

I had been a little farther away from it, and I had felt it. It could have hurt me. I could only imagine what it would have done to her, and I didn't like it. "I started it. The game. I filled the marbles with magic and started throwing them like bombs. It's my fault."

"Aurora threw the last one. If I were to blame someone, it would be her." Thea rested a hand on my arm. "I'm fine, Keeran. Don't be so hard on yourself."

I took a step back and repeated, "Easier said than done."

"Keeran—"

I cut Drake off. "It's okay. I'm fine." What a freaking lie. "I just need ..." I gestured to the mansion. "I'll see you later."

"Keeran, wait," Thea called to me as I walked away.

"Thea," I heard Drake said. "I think he wants some time alone. We'll talk to him later."

I sped up my steps and veered to the west side of the mansion, where I found an old servants' entrance—it was less used and less likely to have any witches around—and made my way in.

I did my best to keep my mind optimistic, thinking Thea and Drake were right. I shouldn't listen to the other witches, even if ninety-nine percent of them were against me. I shouldn't care.

Easier said than done, I thought to myself again. That seemed like my life's motto lately.

Even using less frequented routes, I couldn't escape them. I was walking down a corridor, trying to get to the stairs that would lead me to the second floor, where my room was, when I heard them.

"I don't understand how Thea doesn't see that warlock is a menace," Alma said.

"To her, to her daughter, and to us!" Dinah said.

Several other voices spoke up in agreement. There were more witches with Alma and her troupe now.

Despite my will to move on, I stopped feet from the archway leading to a sitting room and listened.

"We need to do something," Dinah said. "If Thea can't see the threat that warlock is, then we have to show her."

"I agree with you," another witch said. "But I would rather not anger Thea. If she says she trusts him, shouldn't we try to do that too?"

"Are you crazy, Edith?" Alma practically shouted. "He's an aberration. An evil being who was supposed to die years ago. He has to be eliminated."

"I'm with Edith," a fourth witch said. "If Thea finds out we did something, she'll punish us. Besides, haven't we all agreed she's working for the best of our coven? Of every coven?"

"When you forget she's mated to a vampire," Alma spat. "Then yes, I believe she has everyone's best interest at heart."

"Then trust her judgement," Edith said.

A moment of silence passed. "We'll see," Alma said. "For now, I'll keep my eye on that warlock. I don't trust him."

My chest constricted with anger and frustration and depression. Before I could let my emotions get the best of me,

I retraced my steps and turned down another corridor, taking a longer path to my bedroom. Thankfully, I didn't encounter any more witches on my way, so I was able to keep my calm until I locked my bedroom's door behind me.

Once inside, I cast a shield over my door and windows and screamed. I screamed until I felt my fury fade. No, not fade. Just retreating. Calming down a little. Hiding behind other feelings. Waiting for another time to strike.

After I had that out of my system, I dropped the shield and crossed the room. I opened the window and took a deep breath.

Because of my shameful upbringing—serving as not only a slave for the witches, but a sex toy for many of them—they saw me as weak. And now they thought I was a threat because they had been taught to kill any male born from a witch, believing warlocks would bring evil and destroy the witches. I didn't want to care what they believed, but it was hard to argue when the few warlocks who had survived to adulthood had indeed attacked witches.

I preferred they view me as weak, lest they knew all the rage and scars that I carried inside me. I tried my best to keep it all in, to disguise it with quietness and reclusion, but until when? Every time something like this happened, I could see myself exploding, letting out my magic and hurting them for real.

Perhaps warlocks were evil beings. That was the only explanation I had for my dark thoughts and emotions.

Maybe they were right to be afraid of me.

What if I was a threat to Thea, Aurora, and the other witches?

Perhaps I should leave.

On the horizon, the sun was halfway through its descent,

staining the sky orange and pink. Summer was ending, which meant the sunset was earlier and the night air was crisper.

Soon, the moon would be up.

Every time I saw the moon, I thought about Luana. Drake and Thea received weekly updates from her, and they had even gone to visit her twice in the last year. She had come two or three times for a quick stop too. Her pack was having difficulties accepting her as its new alpha.

Perhaps she could use a hand.

I perked up, liking that idea. Here, I was hated and threatened. It was only a matter of time before the witches rallied together and forced me to leave or killed me. Who knew how I would react, how my magic would react if that happened? I didn't want to hurt anyone, especially Thea, Aurora, and Drake.

But in the Dark Vale pack, I would be a stranger. I could pretend to be a diplomat sent by Drake to check on things. I didn't need to do anything other than support Luana.

Before the excited feeling of purpose fled, I marched to my closet and picked up a large duffel bag.

But, as I reached for my shirts, my hands froze. The feeling of purpose left me.

Could I spend time with Luana and keep a secret from her?

The couple of times I had seen her since the DuMoir battle, I had to literally bite my tongue several times. The guilt and shame over what I had done, over what Drake and I had done, weighed on me. I wished I could tell her, but I knew, I just knew, that once I did, our friendship would disappear. She would hate me. She would despise me. She would never want to see me, or Drake, again.

When we came up with the plan to have Luana kill Ulric

and gain the control of the pack, so she could order them to help us during the battle, Drake and I trusted she could do it. But it turned out Ulric was stronger than anyone anticipated. He was about to kill Luana, and in that moment, I didn't think. In that moment, I didn't care about having the pack on our side, about winning the battle; I just couldn't imagine Luana dead. So, I acted. I used my magic and intervene in the fight, helping Luana kill Ulric.

As far as Drake and I knew, no one besides us knew what I had done. Luana didn't even suspect. And if she did, she would kill us. Because the alpha challenge was a sacred thing. A wolf had to win fairly, without any outside help. Otherwise, it was a violation of their rules. As punishment, that wolf would be banished from the pack—something worse than being killed.

Drake and I had made her a rule breaker. If she ever found out, if her pack ever found out, I didn't even want to think about it.

No, I would never be able to spend a couple of days, much less weeks or months, with Luana. My consciousness would never allow me to keep such a big secret from her. Even if it meant she would never talk to me again.

I didn't want to lose Luana as a friend.

Thus, I dropped the duffel bag and went back to my room, where I plopped down on my bed and wished for better days.

3

LUANA

This wouldn't do. I wouldn't hide in my cabin, afraid of what might happen. I was the damn alpha, for goodness sake.

But, as much as I wanted to fight it, Patricia had a point. Maybe, just maybe, finding a mate could help me. If I had a strong wolf beside me, and eventually pups—I shuddered at the prospect of getting hitched and becoming a mother and *not* for the right reasons—I could control the reins of my life and guide the pack with a firm hand. Together with Drake and Thea, we would make the supernatural world thrive in peace.

I didn't know how I would find a mate.

I knew where, though.

After having a light lunch and making sure I looked respectable in my leather pants and suede tunic, I strode out of my cabin and went to the river that ran through the forest just behind the village. Summer was almost gone, but it was still hot enough for a swim, and with werewolves being naturally hotter than any other creature, we sometimes needed a good cold bath to calm us down. On this particularly hot day, I was sure most of the wolves would be taking a break by the river.

As I sat down atop a rock formation a few feet from the river, where I had an advantageous view of the area, I confirmed my suspicion had been right. At least three-fourths of the pack was here and more than half of them were in wolf form, playing in the cold water.

The wolves probably thought I was keeping an eye on things. Little did they know I was looking for a possible mate.

I let out a long sigh.

This task seemed ridiculous, but I had no other plan.

So, I looked from male wolf to male wolf, waiting for the mating bond to slip into place.

The first one my eyes found was Charles. Not too tall, but wide and strong. He wasn't the most handsome man out there, but he wasn't bad either. Although, his personality killed the mood. The wolf thought he was a gift sent from the skies, and because of that, he bullied everyone.

Beside him was Roy. The tall, lean wolf was younger than Charles, but also ten years older than I was. His biggest negative points: He liked to gossip as much as Patricia.

On the other side of the river, I found Elmer. If I was being honest, Elmer was good looking, but he wasn't strong. I needed a strong wolf by my side.

Then there was Isaac. In terms of looks, he rated close to Charles. He was strong, but he was also a womanizer. He liked to have a different woman every week. Even though I was searching for a mate because of pack politics, I wanted my partner dedicated to me and only me.

Burke, Tripp, Morton, Abe. The list went on and on. But nothing happened. All I knew about the mating bond was what I had been told from others. If a wolf was close enough to his mate, shared a touch, or had sex, the bond would snap like a taught cord pulling at the wolf's heart. However, I had also heard of wolves who felt the bond take simply by looking into their mate's eyes. That was what I was hoping would happen, since I didn't feel inclined to touch, or have sex, with each male wolf in the pack in search of my mate.

Moon be damned, this was ridiculous. I would never find a mate like this. I wished I would have one of those magical experiences where I fell in love with the wolf destined to be my mate. I wanted to feel attracted to him *before* mating.

Was that too much to ask?

It seemed like it was. I guess I had to find another way to secure my position.

From here, I could see Wyatt in the water with his friends —other teenagers who were eager to prove themselves. Wyatt had been a good ally since I had donned the alpha mantle, and he was a handsome young man. With dirty blond hair, dark green eyes, tanned skin, and a strong physique, he would be a handsome adult. It was a shame he was too young.

Right at the edge of the water, Patricia caught my attention. As if sensing me, she glanced at me, her eyes meaningful. And moon be damned, I knew exactly what she was trying to say. *Choose Charles.* I could practically hear her voice in my mind as if we were in wolf form. I did my best to not act like a teenager myself and roll my eyes at her.

She couldn't be right. I couldn't force a mating bond with Charles. There had to be another way.

A new scent reached my nostrils, and I stiffened.

It was a new scent, but it was also an old one.

I shot to my feet, staring at the line of trees to my right. A second later, the rest of the pack picked up on the scent and turned to the newcomers.

Strolling like a goddamn queen, Isalia emerged from the forest, followed by seven wolves.

She stopped in the middle of the pack and her dark eyes met mine. She wore a crude leather dress over her voluptuous body, and her long, unruly black hair flowed behind her with the gentle breeze. "Luana," she said, smiling at me.

My name on her lips brought little goose bumps to my arms.

Isalia had been Ulric's mate. After I killed him and became alpha, she upped and left, without any explanation. The rumors had spread that she was so upset over her mate's death that she couldn't stay in the pack anymore, she would rather become a lone wolf than remain here.

But she had returned and she wasn't alone. The seven wolves with her were the ones who had put up a fight my first week as alpha. They had called me names, insulted me and my deceased parents, and a couple of them had even challenged me. After I defeated them, they wouldn't let it go. Whispers that they were raising a rebel force reached my ears, and when I interrogated them and they refused to divulge anything, I had banished them.

To a wolf, banishment was worse than death, but I didn't want to be the alpha who killed at every opportunity. Besides, despite the sick feeling in my gut, I knew their punishment would serve as a good example to the other wolves who wanted to rebel against me. So, I cast them away.

And now, they had joined forces with Isalia. Why wasn't I surprised?

Slowly, I jumped down from the rock formation and

approached Isalia and her gang. "Why are you here?" I asked, my voice firm.

Isalia tilted her head. "Is that the way to greet a fellow pack member?"

"You left on your own accord." I pointed to the wolves behind her. "And these seven were banished. I'll give them five minutes to leave before I'm forced to do something more drastic."

Isalia took a step closer. "And do what? Kill them? From what I've heard, you don't have the guts to kill anyone." She gestured to the wolves standing with her. "You couldn't kill them. And when Charles challenged you yesterday, you didn't kill him." At that Charles rose to his feet. I tried swallowing the surprised gasp that rose to my throat when he stood beside Isalia, but I was sure they all had heard it nonetheless. "Which tells me, you don't have what it takes to be alpha."

My brows curled down. "Charles, what are you doing?"

He stuffed his chest. "Choosing a side."

"W-what?"

"Luana of the Dark Vale pack," Isalia spoke louder. "I challenge you to a duel. A fight for the alpha position."

My stomach dropped. I wasn't expecting this today. Especially not from her and a gang of banished wolves—they should have been hundreds of miles from here.

I lifted my chin and said the only thing I could, "I accept your challenge."

My heart beat wildly, and I was sure every wolf around the river knew how nervous I was.

The pack wolves retreated, forming a circle around a good portion of grass between the river and the trees, leaving the space free for the duel. In the middle of the circle, Isalia began undressing.

Wyatt stood beside me. "You can do this," he whispered. He put his arms out, palms up, waiting for my clothes.

I slipped off my pants and tunic and underwear, and gave them all to Wyatt. Then I shifted. Instantly, my sight and my hearing increased in quality. I could hear Isalia's bones cracking and her muscles stretching from the inside as she too shifted.

In her big, gray wolf form, she faced me.

Goddamn it, she was big for a female wolf. She wasn't that much bigger than me in human form, was she?

Patricia, as the self-appointed mediator, stepped into the clearing. "You two know the rules." She glanced between the both of us. "Fight until you can no more. Until you're seriously injured or dead." She raised her arm. "Ready?" Isalia snapped her teeth, indicating she was ready. I let out a short howl. Patricia dropped her hand. "Begin!" She quickly retreated to the circle of spectators.

The next second, Isalia lunged at me.

Again, I had to play the speed game. I would only win here if I was faster than her. When Isalia was a foot from me, I jumped to the side, then forward, putting some distance between us.

"That's what she does best," Charles yelled from the crowd. "She runs away!"

I let out a snarl, aimed both at him and Isalia. I wasn't running away; I was strategizing. At least, as much as I could before Isalia got the best of me.

As I expected, Isalia came at me again. These damn duels were always the same. Charge, evade, charge, evade.

This time, when I sidestepped her and angled my body, ready to do with her what I did with Charles the other day, something sharp scratched my snout. Had it been her claw? Her teeth? I hadn't seen those near my face.

The scratch burned, sending rippling pain down my neck. My vision became fuzzy. By the moon, what the hell was this?

I blinked, clearing my sight, and found Isalia with her lips curled back, like she was smiling.

Ready to fall? she asked in my mind.

What did that mean?

She came for me again. Tired of this game and feeling like I was suddenly getting too tired too fast, I met her halfway. I twisted the moment we met and bit down on her shoulder. However, my fangs only scratched her before she ducked down and threw her paw at me, scratching my side. This time, there was pain, but not the burning and the dizziness. Whatever she did before when she scratched my snout had been different.

I retreated as she let out a ringing laugh in my head.

The burning in my snout increased and I blinked again, trying to get my head straight.

What did you to me? I asked, but as I expected, she didn't answer.

She lunged at me.

It took me a moment to recover and move and that moment cost me. Isalia barreled into my side and pushed me down, pressing her paws and digging her nails on the wound on my side and on my snout. I yelped as the pain spread through my muscles, taking my strength away.

No, no, no, not yet.

Isalia curled over me and then a long, thin blade appeared in her mouth, a blade covered in bluish liquid. My eyes widened in terror as she plunged that blade into my side, pushing it deep.

I howled as a burning pain started deep within me, bringing dark spots to my sight and tremors to my already weak muscles. I felt whatever that blue liquid was spreading through my veins.

When I thought I couldn't endure more, Isalia closed her mouth around the wound, making it wider, bigger. Disguising the knife cut.

I was halfway out of mind and barely noticed as the weight of her paws disappeared and she retreated a few steps.

Patricia approached, eyeing from a good distance, and Wyatt rushed to my side.

"Luana?" Patricia asked. I tried to howl, to yelp, to utter some kind of sound, but all I could do was focus on breathing, because even that was too damn hard now. With a solemn expression, Patricia gestured to Isalia. "To the new alpha."

As if her words ignited the magic binding us, I felt as the power shifted. It slipped away from me and traveled to Isalia. Instantly, I could feel she was my alpha now. More than the pain assaulting my body, sorrow dragged me down.

The new alpha shifted back into her human form. With a wide smile, she stuffed her naked chest and faced the pack. "It's my pleasure to become your new, *true* alpha."

Whispers and some cheers came from the crowd, but I didn't pay much attention as Wyatt's hands hovered over my body. "Luana? Are you okay? Talk to me!" Gathering whatever little strength I still had, I shifted back to my human form. Wyatt cursed under his breath. "It's bad, Luana. This is bad."

"S-she ..." I inhaled deeply, fighting against the pain and the dizziness. Moon be damned, it *hurt*. Everything hurt and burned.

"Save your energy," Wyatt said. Then he spoke louder, "We need a healer!"

"No!" Isalia said, loud and clear. "From this moment on, Luana isn't a Dark Vale wolf any longer. She doesn't have a right to our healers or anything else from our pack."

"But—"

"She cheated," I rasped. Through gritted teeth, I pushed against the ground and was able to sit up. Blood dripped down my side and pooled under me. "S-she had a knife." Each word I uttered was like a new stab, but I had to do it. "And the knife had some kind of poison." I gritted my teeth. "I can feel it inside me, weakening me."

"Blade?" Patricia stared from me to Isalia.

Isalia opened her arms and spun around. "As you can see, I don't have any blades."

Wyatt searched around me. "I-I don't see any blade around here."

"I didn't have any blade," Isalia said, calm and absolute. "She must be imagining things from the blood loss." She indicated the red stained ground I was sitting near. "Thankfully, her wounds aren't lethal. Soon her healing will kick in, and she'll be fine." She turned her eyes to me. "But since you've been banished, you better leave."

Wyatt grabbed my elbow and helped me up. A wave of vertigo hit me and I had to lean against the young wolf before I fell back to the ground. "I know what I saw. You cheated."

Charles stepped to Isalia's side. "I didn't take you for a

sore loser. Just put your tail between your legs before we make you leave."

"Or worse," Isalia snarled. Right now, she seemed eager to kill me. Then why didn't she?

Wyatt tugged at my elbow. "Luana, go." He pushed my clothes into my arms. "Please, just go."

I stared at Wyatt's worried eyes, to Patricia's sad ones, then to the rest of the pack. All of a sudden, my life spun out of control. It slipped through my fingers like sand.

The seven wolves I had banished before came to stand behind Isalia. They bared their sharp teeth at me. That was my warning.

Taking a long, painful breath, I raised my chin and spun around. I didn't put my tail between my legs like Charles wanted me to. Even though I was limping and my muscles didn't obey me as they should, I walked out of the clearing with pride.

Isalia had cheated. She had taken the pack from me and she hadn't killed me. That was her mistake. Because I would be back for her, and next time, it would be her doom.

4

KEERAN

I CALLED MY POWER. IT QUICKLY ANSWERED, MY VEINS thrumming with its energy. I held it in, molding it inside me, feeling it.

One thing Thea always said during our practice sessions was that if I wanted to have more control over my magic, I had to get used to it. She and the other witches had been born into this coven. They had been practicing magic since they first showed their powers, usually at the age of five. But me? I was twenty-four and had had powers for about eighteen months. Despite seeing the witches casting spells all my life and remembering one useless spell here or there, I didn't know anything.

But I couldn't keep hurting the people around me, especially Thea and Aurora. I had to learn to control my magic more if I was going to be around them. So, I lied to Thea, and told her I wasn't feeling well. I skipped our morning lesson, only to come to a hidden corner of the back gardens, near the edge of the forest, to practice alone.

Until I could safely say I would never unwillingly harm anyone again, I would train by myself, even if it ended up taking longer this way.

Better safe than sorry.

My power pumped inside me, asking, begging for release. I inhaled deeply and clenched my hands, willing my magic to withdraw. To pull back, even if just a little. I focused on my power, imagining it was a river inside my body. I opened an invisible faucet and demanded it to go through, channeling it. Slowly, the magic receded. First, it lowered to eye level. I took another deep breath and squeezed my fists tighter. The water receded to my lips. Painfully slow, it kept going down.

But it got stuck in my throat. As if it was really water inside me, I coughed, suddenly having a hard time breathing. My knees bent and I leaned forward, clasping my throat as I coughed again.

The power surged up inside me.

I only had time to extend my hands in front of me before it went flying from my palms in two thick red rays. My eyes widened as I took in the patch of grass where the rays hit several feet from me. The green lawn had been burned to a crisp and smoke wafted off it.

Freaking, cursed powers of mine.

"I see you still haven't gotten control of your powers." Her voice, dripping with fake sweetness, made the hairs on my neck stand on end. "I should have recorded it and showed it to Thea. She would certainly agree with me and kill you on spot. Or at least, banish you from our coven."

I closed my eyes for a second, trying to calm down. I only gave myself two seconds, before I turned around and faced her.

Wearing a long black gown with red details, Giselle stood a good ways from me, two other witches flanking her.

"Beat it, Giselle." Her name brought a sour taste to my tongue.

The corners of her lips tipped up. "Ah, Keeran. Don't be so harsh. It wasn't long ago when we enjoyed some good times together." I flinched, doing my best to *not* remember anything. "Don't be mad at me. I'm looking out for my coven. However ..." She took a step closer and her eyes ran the length of me. "We can still have some fun before Thea kicks you out."

Back when I was a slave for the Silverblood witches, Giselle had been one of the witches to use me—to abuse me. At least once a month, she ordered me to her room and—

I shook my head, pushing those thoughts away.

"In your dreams," I spat.

Losing her smile, Giselle waved her hand toward me. Magic enveloped me, tying my wrists and ankles. "If you fight it, we can do it the hard way."

I jerked against the magic, but it only tightened, pulling my arms to my sides and my legs apart. "Let me go, you sick witch."

She strolled to me. "Or what?" She ran her finger up my chest and around my shoulder. "So you can go running and crying to mommy Thea and tell her that mean kids hurt you?" She rose to her tiptoes, and leaning into me, whispered in my ear, "Don't resist and I won't hurt you."

As if. I jerked hard against her magic, but the only thing it did was hurt my wrists and ankles more. "You cursed—"

"Do you remember June and Irene?" she asked, cutting me off. She gestured to the other two witches watching us. "I don't think they ever played with you. But after seeing you walking around the mansion, they were intrigued. After all, you are a handsome man, Keeran." Giselle beckoned the other witches forward. As they approached, Giselle laid her hands on my chest. "Relax. Just close your eyes, and remember all the fun we used to have."

I closed my eyes, but it was to try to push those memories away. What did they think? Just because I was a man I wanted sex all the time? And like this? These witches disgusted me. If they never laid a finger on me again, it would be perfect.

Unfortunately, the damage of being abused by them for years was embedded in my core. For the last eighteen months, I had been free of their torment, but not from the nightmares and the panic that attacked randomly. I could never forget how those cursed witches tied me up and used my body as it pleased them.

Knots formed in my stomach.

Back then, I thought I was human and my physical strength never had a chance against their magic. But now? Now I had freaking magic of my own.

I channeled my power once more, this time without restraint. I filled my veins, my core, my body. Then, when Giselle's hand slid down my chest, aiming south, I screamed and let it all out.

Giselle yelped as she and her friends flew several feet back and landed on their butts. Their hair was messy and dresses were crumpled as if they had touched a high voltage powerline; they stared at me as if I had broken some sacred rule.

The rage and frustration were back in my chest, driving my actions. Driving my magic.

Giselle shot up and smoothed down her gown. "Who do you think you are?"

"You'll soon find out," I said through gritted teeth. Big red bolts appeared on my hands. "Or maybe you'll be dead and won't." I aimed.

"Keeran."

The magic flickered and the bolts disappeared from my hands. I glanced down at my palms, realizing what I had almost done. Holy shit, I had let my emotions get the best of me and had almost killed Giselle and her friends.

Shame quickly replaced the anger and frustration, and I hid my hands behind my back as Elisa, Thea's second, approached us.

"A-are you looking for me?" I asked, my voice a little shaky.

Elisa glanced from me to Giselle, then back to me. "What's going on?"

"Nothing," I said quickly.

From the gleam in her eyes, I could see Elisa didn't buy it, but she didn't push it either. "All right, Keeran, Thea is looking for you. Please come with me."

My stomach tightened. Thea was looking for me? Had she heard what I had done here? But how? It had been seconds ago? Who had told her? Had Giselle planned this? Was this her plan to make Thea see, to finally know how evil I could be and send me away? Or worse, kill me?

I took a deep breath, calming my racing mind, and without another glance at the wicked witches, I followed Elisa back to the castle. Instead of bringing me to Thea's study, Elisa guided me to the corridor on the third floor. Thea stood at the end, staring at the closed door in front of her.

"He is here, my queen," Elisa said, lowering her head.

Thea blinked then nodded at Elisa. "Thank you. You can go now." Elisa bowed once more, then marched down the corridor. Thea's blue eyes landed on me. Squinting, she tilted her head. "I sense magic crackling from you. What happened?"

So, she didn't know anything. I wasn't sure if that was good or bad, but it gave me a choice. Should I tell her all about what had happened or hide it and hope Giselle and her gang didn't utter a word?

Thea, the only person who had ever talked to me as if I was an actual person. The one who had given me hope and saved me. The one who brought me into her family and treated me like a brother. How could I lie and hide something from her?

"You're not gonna like this," I said. Then, I told her everything. I didn't spare one detail. I told her how Giselle had abused me for years, that she had been tormenting me since we had moved back to the Silverblood mansion a year ago, how she had found me and tried to immobilize me and use me again. I even told her I lost control of my temper and my magic. If Elisa hadn't gotten there when she did, I would have either killed Giselle, or hurt her badly. "I'm ... I'm ashamed of my actions. I'm sorry."

Thea rested her hand on my arm. "Keeran ... Of course, I'm not happy about your reaction, but it wasn't your fault. Anyone would have lost control and attacked in turn. I know I would. The ones who are in trouble here are Giselle, June, and Irene. I'll talk to them, punish them if necessary, but not right now." Her expression fell.

Nowadays, it was rare to see Thea sad. "What is it?" I asked.

"It's Bagatha. She's dying."

I sucked in a sharp breath. "W-what?"

The first Queen of All Witches was old, over a thousand

years old, and she was powerful. Well, she had been, until she used the last of her magic to help Drake save Thea's life. Since then, she had been looking more like an old human woman at the end of her life. Still, I never believed she would die one day.

Thea reached for the knob. "She asked to see you."

I stared at Thea, a little taken aback, as she opened the door and entered the room.

Bagatha had asked to see me? Why?

It took me a moment to follow Thea inside. I closed the door and crossed the sitting room, all the while my eyes remained locked on the frail figure lying in bed.

Thea sat in a chair beside the bed and held Bagatha's hand. "Bagatha, can you hear me?"

Bagatha opened her eyes. "Yes. Is he here?"

"Yes, I've brought Keeran as you asked." Thea gestured for me to approach the bed. I swallowed and stood a foot behind Thea. "He's right here."

Bagatha's unfocused eyes traveled from Thea to me and a chill ran down my spine. If I were to guess, the old witch's sight wasn't the same as it once was. She let go of Thea's hand and beckoned me. "Come closer, warlock."

I took a step closer, my knees touching the side of the bed. "I'm here."

She gripped my arm and pulled me down—for an old, dying woman, her grip was still strong. I sat down on the bed beside her. She didn't let go of my hand as she said, "I have something to tell you." Her voice was thin and feeble. "I wish I could have told you sooner, but I feared you weren't ready. Truth be told, I still think you aren't. But now I have no choice."

That piqued my curiosity. "What are you talking about?"

"Keeran," she started, but her words were interrupted by a raking cough. Gently, Thea lifted the old witch's head and helped her drink a little bit of water. All the while, my insides were in knots. What the hell did she want to tell me? When Thea laid the old witch back down, Bagatha inhaled deeply and tried it again. "Keeran, your mother is alive."

Beside me, Thea gasped.

I stared at the old witch, my brain frozen and unable to process what she had said.

"How is that possible?" Thea asked.

"You have to find her, Keeran," Bagatha continued, ignoring Thea's question. "She's in peril." My breath caught. "You need to find her and help her. Otherwise, she'll perish, and an entire coven of warlocks will be lost."

If I wasn't seated, I would have fallen down. "A-are you saying I'm not the only warlock alive? There's an entire coven of them?"

Bagatha started saying something, but another round of coughing interrupted her. Thea tried lifting her up again, but Bagatha slapped her hand away. "It's almost time ..." she wheezed. "Let me finish." Time for what? "Keeran, you need to seek the Wildthorn coven. They will be able to help you."

"The Wildthorn coven?" I asked, confused. They were a coven of witches. I thought she was going to point me toward the warlock coven.

"They will have answers," Bagatha rasped. "Now ... it's time."

Thea's eyes filled with tears. "Is there anything I can do for you?"

"No, my dear." Bagatha's voice was a thin whisper. She closed her eyes. "All you have to do now is raise Aurora well, guide her, and help her become the best Queen of All Witches the world could ever have."

A tear slid down Thea's cheek. "I will. Thank you ... for everything."

Closing her eyes, Bagatha inhaled deeply.

And then, she stopped breathing all together.

I shot to my feet. Wait? When she said it was time ... it was about her death? When Thea told me Bagatha was dying, I thought she meant the old witch still had a few days, or a few hours at least, not mere minutes. I never would have thought she was literally dying.

Thea covered Bagatha's body with a white blanket, up to her shoulders, then she caressed the old witch's face. I didn't know what to do or say. I hadn't had much contact with the former Queen of All Witches, aside from the couple of times she had helped Drake and Thea, and when she came to visit the mansion every two to three months. Last month, when she came to visit, she stayed—I guess she knew she was dying then. Ever since then, I rarely saw her around the mansion.

And now she had dropped not one but two huge bombs in my lap ... and died.

I stared at her serene face. Like this, she seemed to be only sleeping. My heart squeezed.

Wiping her tears from her face, Thea turned and faced me.

"Did you know about that?" I asked, before she could say anything. "About my mother *and* a warlock coven?"

She shook her head, her golden hair swaying side to side. "No, I didn't." She clasped my arms. "But don't you see? This is an opportunity."

"Opportunity?"

"If the events from this morning are any indication, things

around here will only become worse. I'm trying to protect you the best I can. I'll punish Giselle, June, and Irene, and show the others what happens when they hurt you, but you know witches. They are a crazy, unstable bunch." She grimaced. "Unfortunately, I can't guarantee something like this, or worse, won't happen again."

I took a step back and stared at her. "What are you saying?"

"Don't you want to look for your mother and the warlock coven?"

"I do ..."

"Then, that's an order," Thea said. "As your queen, I order you to go on a mission: Seek out the Wildthorn coven and find your mother and the warlock coven." Even though that was what I wanted to do, having Thea send me away like this? It hurt. "Keeran, you know I'm sending you on this mission to protect you, right?"

"Right," I muttered.

"How does that saying go? Two birds with one stone? You stay away from all the hurt this place brings you, and you look for your mother and others like you. It's a win-win."

When she put it like that, It didn't sound so bad. "All right ..." I glanced around, suddenly feeling lost. What time was it? What day? Wait, what about Bagatha and her funeral? "When should I leave?"

Thea's answer was absolute. "Now."

5

LUANA

Because of my wounds, I dragged myself for five miles, a reasonable distance from the pack, and stopped for a breather. While fleeing, I could feel whatever damn poison Isalia had used in her blade, making my muscles tight one second and like a dead worm the next. I either tripped because my legs couldn't hold me, or because they locked and I couldn't move.

Under the shade of a thick tree, I rested while my healing kicked in, and slowly, my wounds stopped bleeding. It would take a few days for all the cuts and scratches to disappear from my body.

Once my body recovered a little, my thoughts went from my pain to my future. What now? What was I supposed to do? Become a lone wolf living in the woods? Find another pack and try to weave my way through their ranks? Recover and challenge Isalia, just like that?

I didn't know.

Since becoming alpha, I had felt uncomfortable and out

of place. Like I had been forced into the position, when that wasn't the case. Drake hadn't forced me to kill Ulric and become alpha. I had volunteered. Because I thought I could be a great leader like Drake was. As far as I knew, Drake never wanted to be lord of the castle, but when he saw what Alex was doing to the place, how he was destroying not only vampires, but plotting a war with the witches and were-wolves, he couldn't just stand by and watch. He planned and he acted and he stole DuMoir Castle back. Now he was a fair leader.

That was what I wanted to do, who I wanted to be.

But instead of helping my pack, I had been kicked out of it.

The only thing that came to mind was go to DuMoir Castle. I knew that wasn't the best place for a werewolf to live, as the castle was crawling with vampires, but I was sure Drake would let me crash in a guest bedroom while coming up with a plan. Damn, he might even help me come up with one.

After a couple of hours, I pushed up from under the tree, got dressed in the clothes Wyatt had handed me, and marched on, now with a certain destination. My limbs still ached and my wounds still throbbed, but I gritted my teeth and kept going.

I walked through the forest for four hours before deciding I was ridiculous. It was almost nighttime, and it would take me a day to get to DuMoir Castle. I could shift and run in my wolf form, or I could find the nearest road and steal a car.

I would have preferred shifting, but my wounds and muscles still hurt. Only the moon knew how long I would be able to endure running like that. So, I veered south. There should be a town about four miles from here. I was sure to be able to steal a car there—or borrow it, as I planned to leave it on the road near the castle so the owners, or the police, could find it.

Not thirty minutes into my trek, I heard a sound coming up a hill. I held my breath and focused on my hearing. It was a low crushing sound ... what could it be? A wolf? Had Isalia sent one of her supporters to finish the job?

Controlling my breathing so the other wolf couldn't hear it, I stalked through the trees, slinking closer to my prey. The crushing sound came back, near. I ducked behind the bushes surrounding a tree and waited.

I could hear the prey's heart beat and breathing. Whoever he was, he wasn't nervous or concerned. Were all of Isalia's wolves this confident that even when going after a kill, they acted so normal that their heart and breathing didn't change?

Sure he hadn't sensed me yet, I shifted one of my hands into my sharp-clawed paw and jumped over the bush and upon him.

I pushed my prey down to the ground and pressed my claws to his throat.

"Luana?"

Eyes wide, I scooted back. "Keeran? What are you doing here?"

Keeran stared at my arm. "Trying not to get killed?"

"Oh, sorry." I shifted my arm to its human form and looked around. "You're alone? Why?"

Keeran straightened, and that was when I noticed he was garbed in dark leathers and a thin cloak. The last rays of the setting sun bathed his dark brown and face, giving them a golden glow. Shadows highlighted the sharp lines of his face and his warm, brown eyes had a soft edge.

Like this, the tall, wide-shoulder man looked like a powerful warlock.

I remembered the first time I saw Keeran. Drake, Thea, and I had just fled Bagatha's cottage. Wolves from my pack, who were working with Morda, chased after us. We had been badly injured, and Thea was being dragged away, when Keeran appeared out of nowhere and saved us with his power. After that, the lonely warlock had joined our cause and helped us win the DuMoir battle.

But soon after, I had left with my pack while he remained with Thea and Drake. I had barely seen him since.

Keeran gestured to the leather bag at his feet. "I'm on a mission for Thea." His eyes narrowed at my shoulders and face. "Wait, you're hurt." He reached for me.

"I'm fine." I took a step back and waved him off. "Just tell me what your mission is. If you can."

He ran a hand through his hair, pushing the strands back —it had grown a little since the last time I had seen him— then he told me everything. He told me about how Bagatha had told him a secret before dying.

I gasped. "Bagatha? She died?"

"Shit, I forgot you were close to her." He pressed his lips together.

When I was younger, Bagatha had saved me from a hunter's trap. We quickly became friends. It was only much later that I learned her identity—the former Queen of All Witches. And now she was dead.

"Was she okay? I mean, did it hurt?"

He shook his head. "I don't think so. She just seemed tired."

Bagatha had lived a long life. I hoped that for the most

part of her thousand years on this Earth, she enjoyed her stay.

I inhaled deeply, making a note to honor my late friend later, even if it meant performing some burial rituals. If that was the only gift I could give her now, then so be it.

"Go on," I said, my throat dry.

Keeran continued with his tale. Bagatha had called him to tell him to seek out the Wildthorn coven because they would have answers about his mother, who was supposed to be alive and living with warlocks.

"Can you imagine? A full coven of warlocks?"

"Wait ..." I raised my hand, needing a minute. This was too much. "Your mother is still alive *and* there's a coven of warlocks out there?"

He nodded. "I know. It's a lot to take in. But Thea thought I should investigate, so here I am, going to the Wildthorn coven."

I frowned. "You do realize the Wildthorn coven is far from here, right?"

He shifted on his weight. "Yeah. Thea lent me a car, but I had a flat tire about two miles from here. I know there's a small town this way." He pointed to the north. "I was going to either get a new tire, or borrow another car."

It struck me then that Keeran was suddenly alone, engrossed on a mission for himself. I also had a mission in my mind, though I still had no plans for it, but a new idea popped in my head. "We can help each other."

Keeran's thick brows curled down. "What do you mean?"

I sucked in a sharp breath. "I just lost my pack."

His eyes bugged. "What?"

"Ulric's mate challenged me."

"Wait ... I remember Drake mentioned she had left the pack before you returned."

"She had, but I think it was her plan. Leave, gather some help, then return and challenge me." I shook my head. "I couldn't refuse her challenge and I lost. She banished me from the pack."

The pain in his eyes, almost matched the pain I felt inside. "Luana ... I'm so sorry," he whispered.

I didn't want his sympathy. I wanted his help. "We can help each other now," I repeated, eagerness taking hold of my core. "I'll go with you to the Wildthorn coven, and I'll help you look for your mother and this secret warlock coven. After all that is done, you come back with me and help me take down Isalia and her wolves." Keeran looked down and shook his head slightly. "No?"

"That's not it." He raised his head, but his eyes didn't meet mine. "To become alpha again, don't you have to defeat Isalia by yourself?"

"Yes, and I would do that, but I need you to keep her wolves busy," I explained. "What do you say?"

Finally, his eyes locked on mine. "Yeah. Let's do that."

I smiled. I felt like I finally had a purpose. A mission. "Then, let's get to this damned town so we can steal a car and go to the Wildthorn coven." We had no time to lose!

With a new skip to my step, I marched through the forest, with Keeran right by my side. It was odd having him here. It was like we were together to save the world again.

We didn't talk much as we crossed through the forest. The sun dipped behind the trees on the horizon, tinting the sky with purple and dark blue, and we were still three miles from the small town.

"Maybe we should camp here," Keeran said, echoing my

thoughts. We stood in a flat parcel of grass between three thick trees and some tall bushes. "I know it's not as comfortable as if we rented a room at an inn, but ..."

I shrugged. "It's fine. I'm okay sleeping out in the elements." It was my wolf side. I actually loved lying out on the cool grass and looking up the starry sky. My shoulders sagged. "But ... I was kicked out too fast. I didn't have time to grab anything. I don't have any supplies."

"It's okay." Keeran opened his bag. "I should have all we need for one night."

In a silent agreement, Keeran spread out his bedroll and a small towel and the little food he had—I made a mental note to grab more in town tomorrow—while I walked around our campsite, gathering firewood.

When I got back, Keeran had already made a circle with small rocks for the fire. I placed the firewood there and stepped back. Staring at the stack of wood, Keeran flicked his fingers. Fire sparkled and spread through the wood.

"There you go," he said.

"Nice." I sat down on the grass, the fire between Keeran and me.

"You should have my bedroll. I can sleep with my cloak."

I shook my head. "Are you forgetting I'm a wolf? I don't need a bedroll or a cloak."

"I insist," he pushed.

"And I won't argue about this." I understood his desire to be a gentleman, which I appreciated, but this was a silly subject. Groaning, I rolled my shoulder. It was still stiff from the wound. I pulled down the collar of my tunic, trying to get a better look. "Shit," I muttered. It was still red and ugly. That damn poison or whatever Isalia had used must have slowed down my healing significantly. That was the only reason I could fathom why my wounds didn't look better right now.

"What is it?"

"Just … my wounds. They are taking longer than they should to heal." I lifted my tunic and looked at the stab plus bite on my side. This one looked even worse.

With his bag in hand, Keeran scooted to my side. "Let me see."

I pulled my tunic down. "No, it's fine. I'm healing. Slowly, but I'm healing."

Lips pressed tight, Keeran reached for my tunic. "You didn't want to argue about the bedroll, and I don't want to argue about this. Now, remove your shirt and let me see your wounds."

It wasn't like Keeran hadn't seen me naked before. When I had to shift for fights, I stood naked beside him. Sometimes, he even helped me before and after, holding out his cloak for me. And even though I was wearing a sports bra underneath my tunic, this time, it felt different. There was just us here, seated side by side in the dark, no battles raging around us.

Glad he didn't have my enhanced hearing and couldn't listen to the rapid beat of my heart, I slipped my tunic over my head and threw it aside. Keeran leaned over me, hovering his fingers over the wound on my shoulder, then the one on my midriff, unaware that his near touch made my stomach tighten.

He let out a hiss. "They are healing, my ass." He grabbed a small pouch from inside his bag. "Why aren't you healing?"

"Isalia cheated," I confessed. "She used a blade to stab me deep. I think the blade had some kind of poison on it that made my body numb for a while, and is now slowing my healing."

Keeran froze. "She cheated?"

I nodded. "I tried calling her on it, but the other wolves hate me so much, they sided with her anyway."

"That is ..." Keeran grunted. Letting out a long sigh, he opened the pouch and dipped his fingers inside. "I didn't bring many herbs, but this one should help." He looked at me. "This might sting."

He pressed two fingers to the wound on my shoulder, spreading the crushed herb on it. I gritted my teeth and hissed. My hands elongated into claws, and I buried them in the ground, as if I could transfer the burning pain from me.

When he did the same to my midriff, I thought I would faint. What kind of herb was this? Even when I had been seriously hurt before and Thea and Keeran had to use their powers and all kinds of herbs to heal me, it hadn't hurt this much. Well, maybe I had been so out of it that I didn't notice, but this shit *hurt*.

"Are you sure there's no alcohol mixed in with that herb?" I asked, trying to joke, but I was sure the knot in my brows made it look like a threat instead.

"I think it's the poison reacting to the herb," Keeran said, taking a good look. "The herb is burning it away. Hopefully, the wounds will look much better by morning." He sat back and stared at me. "Try to distract yourself. How about dinner? I have some power bars. Sorry, I didn't plan to stop in the middle of the forest, or I would have grabbed something better."

With this pain? "No way can I eat right now." I inhaled deeply, trying to focus on something else. "Tell me something. To distract me. Tell me anything."

"What do you want to know?"

"I don't know. Anything that will take my mind off this

pain. How are Drake, Aurora, and Thea? How about the Silverblood witches? Are they all behaving and accepting Thea as their queen?"

"Drake, Thea, and Aurora are fine. Great even. Watching them together is both great and disgusting. There's too much love going around." Keeran chuckled. "The witches are fine with Thea being queen." Then his amusement fled his face, and his brows slammed down. "But some of them aren't behaving."

He told me how the witches kept asking Thea to either banish or kill him. He couldn't go anywhere without being insulted. And to top it all, he confessed how Giselle, June, and Irene cornered him, binding him with magic. Moon knew what they would have done to him, thankfully his temper exploded and his magic flared up.

He clenched his hands together. "I'm not proud of my reaction."

Enraged, I jumped up to my feet. Pain shot from my shoulder and stomach, making my knees buckle, but I pushed through. "That bitch! Who does she think she is? I'm gonna kill her right now."

I began marching, determined to go to the Silverblood estate and rip Giselle, and her two cronies, into a million pieces.

Keeran shot up and stepped in my way. He grabbed my arms, careful with my wounds, before I could run into him. "It's okay. Thea said she would punish them, and I trust Thea."

"I don't care!" I didn't know why a sudden wave of fury washed over me. Blame it on my hot wolf temper, or on the fact that it was bottled up inside me. Losing to Isalia, being badly hurt, having to walk away, finding out Bagatha had died, and now hearing Keeran had almost been molested by those damned witches. "Thea is too good to kill them, and they deserve to die."

I jerked, trying to get rid of him, but his grip on my arms only tightened. He pulled me closer and looked down on me. The fight fled from me when his eyes locked on mine. "I'm fine, Luana. Really. Forget about them. Let just focus on our missions. That's all that matters now."

Forget about whom? What were we talking about? Because, honestly, how could I think of anything when he was this close, practically looming over me. When the orange light coming from the fire made the sharp lines of his handsome face stand out even more, and his brown eyes glinted in the dark. And his scent ... with my enhanced sense of smell, I was taking the full brunt of his delicious pine and musk scent.

My breath caught and I took a large step back.

Moon be damned, what was happening here? I mean, ever since first laying eyes on him, I had noticed Keeran was handsome. Hot even. And charming. But that was it. No other thought about him had ever crossed my mind, other than fighting by his side and winning that damn war.

Not until now. No, not now. Ever since a few minutes ago, when he was being gentle and treating my wounds.

I cleared my throat and averted my eyes. "Are you sure you're okay?"

He nodded. "I will be. Don't worry." He offered a small smile, which only made my heart race faster.

Moon be damned.

I spun around and grabbed his cloak. After wrapping it around, I nestled under a tree trunk and forced myself to sleep, even though I hadn't eaten anything. "Good night," I said as I lay down and closed my eyes.

"Luana ..." I could hear the irritation on Keeran's voice. "The bedroll. Please, take the cursed bedroll."

"If you didn't notice, I'm already sleeping." I rolled to my side, giving him my back. "Now shut up and go to sleep."

He grunted and from the way his breathing hitched a few times, I thought he would keep bothering me, but Keeran gave in a few minutes later. He slipped inside his bedroll.

But he didn't sleep right away—his breathing hadn't slowed down, and neither had his heart.

I knew the reason I couldn't relax and sleep. Because of the way he had held me and looked at me moments ago.

What was his excuse?

———

WE WERE UP BEFORE THE SUN. IT DIDN'T TAKE A LONG TIME TO pack up.

"I need new clothes," I said, gesturing down to my tunic and pants. There was blood smeared everywhere, and I felt incredibly dirty because of it. "We should continue with your plan of stealing a car in the next town." Then, I could get new clothes and food. With my wolf metabolism, I was always ridiculously hungry—and I had been stupid and not eaten last night. Now, I was dying.

Keeran nodded. "Let's do that."

"Good." I took the lead, veering into the trees and heading to the nearest town.

A few seconds later, a faint snapping sound reached my ears. I froze.

"What is it?" Keeran asked in a low voice.

I turned to him and mouthed, "We're not alone."

His eyes bugged for a brief second, then he extended his hands and channeled his magic.

Not having time for a full shift, I transformed my arms into claws. I jerked my chin in the direction I had heard the snap, and slowly stalked toward it.

But before we could jump our enemy, it stepped out from behind of the bushes and lowered his head.

I gasped. "What in the moon are you doing here?"

THE LIGHT BROWN WOLF WHIMPERED.

"I asked you a question, damn it!" I practically shouted.

Without taking his eyes from the wolf, Keeran asked, "Do you know this wolf?"

I groaned. "Yes, I do. And he's gonna shift into his human form right now before I beat the crap out of him." Slowly, the wolf shifted and a young man stood naked in front of us. He kept his head down. "Now, Wyatt, tell me what the hell you're doing here."

Keeran picked up his cloak from the ground and threw it at Wyatt. The young werewolf caught it. "Thank you," he whispered as he wrapped it around himself. "I'm Wyatt, by the way."

"Keeran," the warlock said, nodding his head in acknowledgment.

"Answer me," I said through gritted teeth.

Wyatt finally looked at me. "I followed you, okay? I left in the middle of the night and followed your trail."

That was insane. "Why? Do you want to become a lone wolf too?" He was too young for that. I appreciated how he had looked up to me while I was alpha, but I wasn't alpha anymore. If he wanted to secure his place in the pack, he had to go back now. "You can't stay here."

"I can't go back either," he said, louder this time.

A new wave of fury took over me. "Don't tell me Isalia kicked you out too?" Shit, if she had, I would rip her throat out.

"No, I sneaked out." He inhaled deeply. "It hasn't even been a day since she became alpha and it was already too much. I couldn't take it anymore." His eyes gained a worried glint. "Isalia is crazy, much more than Ulric ever was. Right after she defeated you, everyone was happy." I flinched. "Sorry," he muttered. "But that didn't last. Isalia started barking orders left and right, telling everyone what to do and when and how. Six wolves stood up to her, telling her she was supposed to be a leader, not an empress. Those six wolves are now dead."

My stomach dropped. "W-what?"

"She killed six wolves because they didn't agree with the way she's running things," Wyatt said. "And that was her first day as alpha. Can you imagine how it'll be after a month?"

"How come nobody has challenged her yet?" Keeran asked. He looked at me. "The other wolves can do that, right? Any wolf can challenge the alpha?"

"Yes," I said in a low voice.

"Yes, but they are afraid of her," Wyatt told us. "She runs around with ten wolves with her, all strong and just as evil as her. Everyone believes now that she cheated to win, so why won't she cheat again if she's challenged? Nobody wants to risk that."

"They prefer bowing to a mad alpha instead?" I asked, though I knew the answer.

"It is that or be killed."

"How about you? How did you escape?" Keeran asked.

"I left in the middle of the night, pretending I was on patrol duty."

I scoffed. "You're too young for patrol duty."

"Right, but I don't think Isalia knows my age, or if she knows, she doesn't care. Anyway, I started patrolling the perimeter, then, when I was at the farthest point of our lands, I ran." He opened a tiny crack of the cloak, showing off the large scratch on his shin. "They noticed I was gone, of course. One wolf caught up to me, but I was able to lose him a couple of hours ago."

I started pacing, my mind racing. "We have to go back. Now. I can't leave the pack like that. I have to challenge her. I need to take her down. She's killing everyone. At this rate, in a month there won't even be a pack. This isn't—"

Like last night, Keeran stepped in my way and grabbed my arms. And once more I was ensnared by him. "Luana, calm down." His voice was gentle, but firm, just like his grip. "Even if you turn around and go back now, what good will that do? You won't be able to defeat her alone, not when she has so many wolves backing her. Not to mention, we know that if you challenge her, she'll cheat again."

"He's right," Wyatt said. "We have to be smart about this. We need an actual plan."

I glanced from Keeran to Wyatt and back to Keeran. "I know, moon be damned, I know. But it hurts." I placed my hand over my heart. "Knowing what she's doing to my pack, it hurts."

Dropping my arms, Keeran nodded. "I know, but you just

have to endure it a little longer." He glanced to Wyatt. "You said the wolves seem to be obeying her right now, right?"

Wyatt nodded. "Yes. They are afraid of her."

"See?" Keeran told me. "She won't kill any more wolves because they are afraid of her and will do her biding for now. We have some time."

"But not long," I muttered.

"True. That's why we're going to Wildthorn now. While we're solving things there, we'll come up with a plan to defeat Isalia. Who knows? If my mother is alive and we find her, I bet she would help us. And if she has some friends, we can ask them to help us too."

I gulped. "That's another war."

"If you ask me, Isalia already declared war the moment she cheated and took the mantle from you," Wyatt said.

Keeran looked down.

I let out a long breath, trying to expel some of the anger building inside me. I knew they were right. We couldn't simply march back to the pack right now. We would be killed in no time, and what good would that do? We needed an actual plan and allies. If this Wildthorn coven and Keeran's mother could help, then so be it.

"Okay." I nodded, feeling like I had been defeated in more ways than one. "We'll go to the Wildthorn coven first."

Keeran returned his eyes to me. "Thank you."

"Don't thank me yet." I crouched and began rolling Keeran's bedroll. "Now help me here so we can get moving."

AFTER BREAKING CAMP, LUANA, WYATT, AND I HEADED INTO town. It was a small village with only a handful of roads and buildings. Since Wyatt had no clothes, he waited at the edge of the forest while Luana and I got our supplies. I went to a store where I bought clothes for Luana and Wyatt, then I found a beat up Jeep without doors parked in a detached garage on a quiet road.

Swiftly, I used my magic to start the Jeep and drove it away. I exited the town and stopped on the shoulder off the main road, where Luana and Wyatt were waiting. I handed them two big bags: one with clothes and other with breakfast.

After Luana and Wyatt got dressed, they hopped into the Jeep, and we had breakfast while I drove west.

At some point, Wyatt drifted to sleep—poor guy was tired after running after Luana all night—and I glanced at Luana, who was staring at the trees, though I doubted she was seeing them.

"What are you thinking about?" I asked, curious.

She turned her face to me, and I made the mistake of glancing at her. The sun streaming from outside hit her just right, giving a golden glint to her hazel eyes and a sun-kissed glow to her skin.

I had always found Luana pretty, beautiful even, but ever since last night, when I held her close, I saw her with new eyes.

Beautiful was a too simple a word for her. Luana was stunning. With her long, light brown hair falling down her back in waves, her bright smile, and her hotter than hell body, she was breathtaking.

She was lively. She was soul. She was fire.

And I found myself totally enthralled by her.

"You know what I'm thinking," she said. "About my poor pack suffering at the hands of that dictator." Her hands clenched into fists. "If only she hadn't cheated. I'm sure I could have won fair and square."

My stomach tightened.

I would burn in hell for hiding the truth from her, but I couldn't tell her now. She was so focused on the fact Isalia had cheated. If she learned that I had helped her cheat when she defeated Ulric, she would kill me.

But now I had a chance to make things right. After we went to the Wildthorn coven, and found my mother and the warlock coven, I would help her. I would go back with her and do everything in my power to help her become alpha again—without cheating.

Then, my lie wouldn't matter anymore and this huge boulder on my shoulders would crumble to dust and disappear.

Without thinking, I reached over and patted her hand on her thigh. "Don't worry. We'll fix it all." Luana stared at my hand on hers. I pulled my hand back and cleared my throat. "Only a few more hours until we're at the coven."

"Tell me if you need to switch. I don't mind driving. But until then ..." Luana sank into the seat and closed her eyes. "I'm going to take a nap."

"How much longer?" Wyatt asked.

Again.

The teenage boy had scored some points in my book when Luana had explained he was a nice wolf, who for some reason was her fan. From what I had detected, it wasn't in a romantic way—because that was the first thing that crossed my mind. He believed in her and wanted her to be alpha. He wanted his pack to be as peaceful as Luana's dreams, and he wanted to help her.

However, he was still a teenage boy. His endurance and strength were supposed to overshadow mine by a mile, and yet he asked if were getting closer every three minutes.

"We don't know," Luana answered, giving me a side glance. She probably thought it was all amusing.

I suddenly felt like a senile old man.

From the directions Thea had given, I knew we were getting closer to the Wildthorn coven, but since I didn't know exactly where it was, I couldn't give him a definite answer.

After driving for most of the day, we left the car on the road—hopefully to be found and returned to its owner—and started hiking through the forest. That was about two hours ago. The farther we walked, the greener and thicker the forest grew, as if the water or whatever made the plants and trees livelier was different here.

I was about to suggest we took a break when Luana and Wyatt stilled. Luana raised her hand, telling me to stop too. Holding my breath, I halted right beside her.

Then two woman jumped from the trees. Wearing green slacks and vests with lines of dark green paint on their cheeks, the two witches stared at us.

"What business do you have at the Wildthorn coven?" one of them asked.

"Finally," Wyatt muttered.

I took a step forward. "I'm Keeran, a warlock, and I'm looking for my mother."

"Your mother?" The one on the right frowned. "What's her name?"

Shit. "I don't know. Bagatha told me I could find her here." I opened my mouth again to tell them about the warlock coven too, but when they exchanged a glance, I pressed my lips tight. One thing at a time.

The witch on the left narrowed her eyes at Luana and Wyatt. "Why did you bring werewolves here?"

"They are my friends," I said. "They are helping me."

Again the witches stared at each other. Then, they stepped aside, creating an opening between them. "This way," the one on the left said, gesturing to the trees behind them.

I stepped past them and through the trees.

Not ten yards later, the trees opened to a valley with lots of trees and houses with brown roofs. Thea had told me the Wildthorn witches practiced earth magic, but I hadn't imagined they lived in what looked like tree houses in the middle of the forest.

"Here." One of the witches pointed to the stone path carved in the valley. "Through here."

"A witch will be waiting for you at the end of the path," the other one said.

I looked at Luana and Wyatt. They seemed okay. Seemingly unafraid that this was a trap or anything weird. So I moved, taking the steps down into the valley, Luana and Wyatt right behind me.

As we went down the narrow path, the trees and houses grew closer and larger. From here, I could see vines winding around the tree branches, colorful flowers sprouting from every corner. The side of the houses were covered by ivy and other kinds of plants. Soon, we were engulfed by the trees and welcomed by another witch at the end of the path.

"My name is Neva," she said. She too was wearing green pants and a vest, but also wrist braces and thick boots. Her long, dark blond hair was tied back in a loose braid and flowers weaved through it. "I'm second to Yira, our Witch Queen."

"I'm Keeran," I said. "A warlock. And these are my friends, Luana and Wyatt. They are werewolves."

"Welcome!" a new voice said. We turned in its direction and I frowned.

A witch walked toward us, wearing a wide smile, a dark green and brown gown, and a crown made of leafs and flowers. "I had a feeling we were receiving visitors this evening."

Neva lowered her head. "My queen."

"Good evening, Queen Yira." I invoked some of Thea's and Drake's diplomacy. "We're—"

Queen Yira waved her hand at me. "I've heard of you. Keeran, Luana, and Wyatt. A warlock and two werewolves. I have to say, what an unusual group."

She said that now, but if she could have seen us a year ago, she would have found our group even weirder. It wasn't everyday a warlock joined a werewolf, a witch, a vampire, and a ghost to save the supernatural world.

Wait. How had she heard of us already? We had only gotten together yesterday. And Wyatt joined us just this morning. I opened my mouth to ask her about that, but Luana acted first.

She bowed her head. "Queen Yira. I hope it's okay that we're here. We're looking for information on a witch, and supposedly, you have that information."

The queen lifted her hand. "Let's talk while we walk. Follow me." She gestured for us to come then marched away.

Without a choice, Luana, Wyatt, and I followed her through the trees. They soon opened up, becoming scarcer, revealing the roads and houses between. These were earth witches, and I shouldn't be surprised, but with their dirt roads, stone paths, wooden houses, and overgrown vegetation, I felt like we had gone back in time, to some kind of 1800s village.

"I've heard about you, Keeran," the queen said as we walked through the roads. Everywhere we looked, we witnessed as witches came out of their homes—women and men and children—all dressed in earth-colored gowns and suits. They bowed to their queen and stared at us with wide eyes. "A human slave from the Silverblood who suddenly found out about his powers."

"It was quite a surprise," I confessed. For some reason, I didn't want to lie to this queen. She knew about my mother—I hoped—and I didn't want to taint my chances. What if I said something wrong? Would she decide I wasn't worth it and kept the truth from me? I had seen that happen too many times before with the Silverblood coven.

"And you helped Thea save your coven from that horrible

Princess Morda." The queen didn't hide the disdain from her sharp face. "I admire that."

"Thank you." On the other side of the queen, Luana caught my eye. She made faces at me, clearly wanting me to push the subject. My gaze drifted around, landing on each witch we walked by. Could one of them be my mother? I cleared my throat. "Queen Yira, we're here because I'm looking for—"

"You arrived on a special day," the queen said, turning and facing us. We quickly halted. "We're preparing a ceremony tonight to honor the Earth." She stepped to the side, giving us a good view of the clearing behind her.

Vines with flowers stretched from tree to tree, covering most of the clearing. Tables were placed to the right, lots of food and drinks covered them. On the left, the space was quickly filling with arriving witches.

With the sun setting, the place glowed golden. Light came from crystal balls hung from the trees around the perimeter. I stared at the closest one, stunned to find moving things inside. As if the magic was several fireflies, bringing light to the clearing.

"That's great," Luana said. I could hear in her tight voice how her temper was shortening. "Thank you for sparing a few minutes to talk to us."

The queen tilted her head. "I don't think I made myself clear. I'm about to attend the ceremony, and I won't answer any of your questions tonight. Please, enjoy the ceremony. Later, Neva will guide you to our guest quarter where you can rest."

She stepped away.

"Wait," I called. The queen paused. "Queen Yira, it's just a few questions—"

The queen's smile turned sour. "Dear Keeran, you're welcome to stay and enjoy the ceremony, but if you bother me with any questions, I'll have to reconsider." I swallowed my protest. "Tomorrow morning, I'll answer all the questions you might have. For now, have fun and rest."

Just like that, she walked away from us, joining the party.

Luana gawked at her. "What a bitch," she whispered, a bite in her words.

"Shh," I said, looking around. No one else seemed to have heard her, which was a relief. Although I was disappointed about having the bad luck of arriving as important ceremony was about to start, I didn't think Queen Yira was a bitch. Her coven was more important to her than uninvited guests. "We should ..." I glanced around again. Men and women and children gathered around the clearing, without a noticeable pattern. They chatted, laughed, drank, and ate. Then, music filled the air, a sound of strings and piano that came from invisible speakers spread around the place ... or magic. They all looked happy and carefree. "I don't know. Join? Ask to go to our rooms now?"

Luana crossed her arms. "I would rather threaten the queen and get answers now."

I didn't know why I thought Luana's rising temper was so amusing, but I suppressed the smile pulling at my lips.

Wyatt frowned. "I think this is the first time I've seen men around witches who aren't slaves."

Me too. I confess I was curious about that. "I wonder if they are all warlocks."

"Why wouldn't they be? Aren't their mothers all witches?" Luana asked.

That was something I planned on asking Queen Yira

tomorrow morning. "All right, I think I'm gonna find Neva and ask her to—"

Half a dozen young witches danced up to us. Holding flowers in their hands, the witches circled around us, then danced between us.

"Hm, what's going on?" Luana asked, distrustful.

"We're welcoming you to our coven," a girl said.

"And to our celebration," another one said.

A young witch hung a necklace of flowers around our necks, another one placed a crown of flowers atop our heads, and another one weaved flowers through Luana's long hair.

"Come on." One of them slipped her hand into Wyatt's and tugged him toward the crowd.

A second one did the same to me. "Wait," I called, but she gripped my hand tight. She only stopped once we were among the crowd.

"Relax." She took my hands and placed one on her waist. "And just dance." I stilled. Wait, dance? At first, I didn't move. But when I looked to my side, I saw Wyatt dancing with a witch, and Luana among several of them. They bumped against Luana and shook her arms, willing her to dance too. A low chuckle escaped my lips. "Your friends are having fun. It's your turn."

Fun. Had I ever had fun? Besides being abused or cowering in a corner as I grew up, all I knew was battle. Even during Thea's and Drake's wedding, a moment of celebration, I didn't relax. How could I when I was in a castle full of the witches who had molested me in the first place?

But here ... this place was hundreds of miles away, and the witches here seemed to be kind to their men. They seemed happy, carefree.

And I was here for a reason. I wasn't hiding in my room

until Thea called me for practice or to spend some time with her and her family. No, I finally had a mission, a mission to find my mother and an entire group of warlocks. I wouldn't be alone anymore.

I let out a long exhale, wishing away all the freaking fear and rage and frustration. Then I let go. I relaxed and let the young witch guide me, practically teaching me how to dance.

After a while, I thought I was getting the hang of it. Then, the witch led me to a large group dancing together and let go of me. A little lost and dizzy from spinning so much, I swayed to the side.

And bumped into Luana.

Her chest pressed to mine; her wide eyes locked on mine.

My breath caught.

She stepped back. "Sorry."

"No, um, it's fine." For some reason, it was more than fine. My hand moved of its own accord, and the words left my throat without consent. "Dance with me," I said, taking her hand in mine.

Her eyes bugged again, but she didn't protest as I pulled her closer and placed my hand on her waist. I could feel the tension in Luana's arms as she placed her free hand on my shoulder.

Imitating the steps the young witch had taught me, I led Luana around the improvised dance floor. Her eyes never left mine and her body was rigid. I bet she was barely breathing.

"Relax," I said, aware I was only repeating the young witch's words.

"I'm not a dancer," she said, her voice tight. "My muscles lock up anytime I try to dance."

I tilted my head and looked at her. Big mistake.

Luana's beauty hit me square in the chest. How could I

have forgotten how striking she was? Just because she had been by my side for the last two days? But I knew I couldn't forget anymore. My fingers itched to trace her smooth chin, her high cheekbones, her straight nose, her full lips. Each line of her face and body were drawn to perfection. And now, with the crown of flowers on her head, giving her a little suavity, I felt myself gravitating toward her. Being pulled by her.

What was this feeling? I had never felt anything like this. All my life, I had been wary of women, especially witches. Until Thea had offered me a friendly hand, I had been treated like trash—and beaten and tortured and abused. Why would I feel anything other than disgust and contempt for them?

But Thea showed me something different. Thea had been a real friend who showed me compassion and sympathy and a good heart. She showed me how a person should treat others. I couldn't change my past and erase those twenty-something dark years. It wasn't easy for me to trust anyone, much less a woman.

Then came Luana. Besides Thea, she was the only one I trusted and considered a friend.

My gaze scanned her beautiful face, trying to commit every inch to memory. I was afraid that, when I closed my eyes, those dark feelings and memories I tried keeping away would resurface, and the beauty I was staring at now would disappear.

I averted my eyes and cleared my throat. "I'm not much of a dancer either." Trying something new, I spun us around a little faster. Luana's feet entangled on mine and we both tripped. We clutched to each other's arms, and by a miracle, didn't face-plant on the ground. "See?"

Luana's lips stretched on a smile. My heart skipped a beat. "We should probably stop dancing before we break something."

I clutched her arms and put them back into place: one hand in mine, and another one on my shoulder. "What if we do? You heal fast, and I can try to use my magic to fix whatever it is."

She shook her head, but didn't resist. She let me pull her close to me, her body just an inch from mine, and guide her through the crowd as we danced the night away.

"ARE YOU NERVOUS?" WYATT ASKED AS WE PACKED OUR THINGS.

Last night after the party, Neva took us to two guest bedrooms—one for Luana, and one for Wyatt and me. Like everything else in this coven, the inside of the rooms had an earthen feel. Rough wooden floors, plants in the corners and crawling over the walls, furniture that seemed to be cut from tree trunks, and curtains and bedsheets with leaves or flower prints. After we showered and rested in the uncomfortable beds—I could swear the mattress was just pine straw put together—we were called early in the morning.

It was time to meet Queen Yira for breakfast.

I glanced at Wyatt. "Not nervous, but anxious." It was true. I didn't have many questions, but my mind was spinning at the possibility of the answers. I was sure the reality was different from whatever idea I had.

Outside, we met Luana.

My heart sped up at the sight of her. She didn't look any different in her leather pants, a vest over a shirt, and boots. Her hair was tied in a loose braid down her back with a few strings of flowers still weaved through the strands. The problem was that Luana was beautiful and stunning always.

I took in a deep breath, willing my heart to calm down. After all, she could hear it. She would wonder why I felt not only anxious, but a little bit nervous.

Nervous because of her.

Neva stood beside Luana. "Are you ready?"

After we assured her we were ready, she guided us down a narrow road that ended in what looked like the largest tree-house in the coven. It wrapped around at least two dozen strong trees, and was three stories tall.

Two witches and two men—I had to ask the queen if they were called warlocks here—guarded the main door. Neva gave them a slight head nod and they moved aside, letting us pass.

We encountered two guards inside the tree house, but to my surprise, Queen Yira was alone on what looked like a mix of porch and sitting room. A round table for six stood to the left, and to the right wooden chairs were turned to the impressive view: the valley went down a little more, revealing a blue lake below. Its surface glowed with the sun shining high, and the green around it was thick and strong.

"Come on in," the queen said, beckoning us to the table. My stomach growled at the sight of so much food. "We can talk and eat." Neva helped the queen to the table, then after we were all seated, she retreated to the wall, like a bodyguard on duty. She didn't think we were here to harm her queen, did she? The queen noticed I was eyeing Neva and said, "Don't worry. She knows you're my guests and won't do anything. But it's her job to keep me safe."

I nodded. "Understandable."

The queen spread her arms, gesturing to the table. "Please, eat."

Wyatt was the first to advance on the food. Luana slapped his hand but joined him soon after. I waited until the queen moved, choosing what she would eat from the abundance of food on the table, before I grabbed some fruit, donuts, and juice.

Wyatt licked his fingers with a loud smack. "This is delicious." He grabbed three more muffins from a tray and dug in.

The queen smiled at him. "Glad you like it." When she turned her eyes to me, though, her smile faded. "You're here to ask questions."

I straightened in my chair. "Yes, Queen Yira."

She waved her hand at me, as if I was a fly in her way. "Then ask."

I glanced to Luana. She gave me an encouraging nod. Clearing my throat, I turned back to the queen of the Wildthorn coven. The witch who apparently held the answers to all of my questions. But first ... "Are all the males warlocks?"

The queen narrowed her eyes. "Not the question I was expecting."

"Neither was I," Luana muttered.

"I know, I just ... I've never seen another warlock," I said. "I came from the Silverblood coven, where the witches used to kill male babies at birth."

"How did you survive?" the queen asked.

That question filled me with dread. If she knew my mother, shouldn't she know that? "I don't know. Bagatha told me my mother was alive and probably here. I figured I would ask her how she did it when I met her."

The queen steepled her fingers over her full plate. "To answer your first question, not all of the men in our coven carry magic. Some of them are humans who fell in love with our witches and chose to live with us, but even the ones who were born from our witches aren't all warlocks. And we chose to stop the barbaric practice of killing the males born with magic many centuries ago. That was one of the many reason we chose to retreat and cut all connection with the Silverblood, Blackmarsh, and Bluemoon covens."

A heavy feeling pushed through my chest. Why couldn't the Silverblood coven think this way? Why did they have to kill the males at birth? What had they been so afraid of? "It changed," I told her, once more thankful for Thea. "The new witch queen of the Silverblood coven is considerate and she won't kill any males."

"I've heard of Thea and her daughter, Aurora, the Queen of All Witches." Queen Yira nodded her head. "In my long lifetime, I've seen plenty of considerate witches and supernaturals turn corrupt. As much as I want to believe the new witch queen and her daughter will be different, I'll have to wait and see. Now to answer your second question, the one you haven't asked yet."

"My mother ..." I whispered.

"Acalla lived here for a short time many years ago," the queen said. Acalla, was that my mother's name? "But Soren and his men found out where she was. She fled to the Bonecrown coven, as she feared it would be the only place where she could be safe."

I frowned. "Who is Soren? And why the Bonecrown coven?"

The queen shrugged. "I'm afraid I can't answer that. If you

seek more answers, then I suggest you go look for your mother at the Bonecrown coven." The queen stood.

"Wait." I shot up to my feet, almost knocking my chair back. "What about the warlock coven?"

"I'm sure Acalla can tell you all about it once you find her." The queen cut her gaze to Neva, who stepped forward. She didn't have any visible weapons, but she might be pointing a sharp sword at our throats with her stoic presence and hard stare. "Neva will show you out now."

That was it? She had called us guests, but she barely let us stay twelve hours, and she didn't answer all of my questions.

To be honest, I had even more questions now.

"Come on," Neva said, pointing to the door.

Without a choice, I followed her out. Luana muttered curses and obscene things under her breath, while Wyatt puffed his chest, also distressed at being handled like a pest that had to be shooed away.

However, my steps faltered when the queen glanced our way and said, "A warning. The Bonecrown coven is made up of witches who practice dark magic. In order to talk to them, you'll need a tribute of blood."

LUANA

THE BONECROWN COVEN WASN'T TOO FAR FROM THE Wildthorn. All we had to do was hike through the woods. It took several hours, but around sundown, I knew we were close. That, or Neva's directions had been misleading.

"I'm not so sure I like this Bonecrown coven," Wyatt said again. This was his new catchphrase for this part of the journey. He had probably repeated it a thousand times since we started the hike.

"Me neither," I said. I had been quiet during the entire journey, my mind on how this mission was turning out to be longer than expected. Meanwhile my pack was suffering at the hands of Isalia.

I was sure Keeran noticed my sour mood, because he kept stealing glances at me, but he didn't say anything.

"What will we do about this blood tribute?" Wyatt asked.

That had been on my mind too.

"Nothing," Keeran said, his voice tight. "If they mention it when we get there, we'll ask what it means." He shook his head. "And then we make a decision."

What did he mean? That if this dark coven wanted only a small drop of blood, he would prick his finger and be done? But what would he do if they asked for a life?

I didn't want to think about it.

The sun was almost down. We wouldn't be able to go on for much longer. If we didn't stumble on the Bonecrown coven in the next fifteen minutes, I would suggest we stopped for the night. Our supplies for camping were limited, but we would make do.

Fifteen minutes passed. Keeran picked up a broken branch, and with his magic, lit a fire at its tip, creating a torch for us. He trudged on, his steps strong and sure. I didn't have the heart to tell him to stop.

Twenty minutes went by.

Twenty-five.

After thirty, I was done. Despite my wolf sight and Keeran's torch, it was too damn dark, and even with my stamina, fatigue and hunger tugged at me. We hadn't eaten properly since breakfast, and my wolf metabolism required a lot of food.

I opened my mouth to tell him, when a sound reached my ears.

I stopped and listened.

Beside me, Wyatt did the same.

Keeran went on for another two steps until he realized we had stopped. He looked over his shoulder at us. "What happened?"

"Shhhhh." Wyatt pressed a finger to his lips.

"Help!" a faint voice said from the distance.

"Someone is asking for help," I told him.

Keeran frowned. "What?"

"A-anybody out there?" the voice called out.

"I don't hear anything," Keeran said.

Of course he didn't. If it weren't for our wolf hearing, Wyatt and I wouldn't have heard it either.

"Help, please!" A sob followed the voice.

Wyatt took off.

"Wyatt!" I called. I cursed under my breath before running after him.

"Luana, wait!" Keeran said as he stayed behind.

If he weren't able to catch up with us, I would come back for him. I just needed to make sure Wyatt wasn't falling into a trap or doing anything stupid.

I sprinted after Wyatt, in the voice's direction, for almost ten minutes. As we ran, the voice and pleas grew louder, more desperate.

Then, it was right in front of us.

A young woman with long silver hair, and slightly pointed ears hung from a tree branch high above.

I blinked at her. "W-what?"

She saw us and another sob cut through her throat. "Please," she begged, her voice weak.

Wyatt climbed the tree and scooted over the branch. I stood underneath the girl, my arms ready to catch her should she fall.

But Wyatt didn't let her. He held on to the rope tied around her chest and pulled it up. When she was within his arm's reach, he grabbed the rope wound around her torso and pulled her up to the branch. She yelped as she swayed over the branch like a pendulum, but with his strength, Wyatt caught her and kept her steady. He scooped her up in his arms and stood on the branch as it creaked.

Whimpering, the girl closed her eyes.

"Don't worry. I've got you," he said.

Then he jumped. He landed on soft knees, but crouched down with the girl.

I didn't think, I just knelt beside them and helped Wyatt tear the rope from her chest, her arms, and her ankles.

This girl was fae.

I had never seen a fae before.

"Are you okay?" I asked. She had bruises and cuts all over her body, and her white dress was torn to pieces and stained with silver—fae's blood. How could she be okay? "What happened to you?"

Wyatt cut me a glare. "She seems to have gone through a lot. Your questions can wait." I stared at him, surprised at his tone. Usually Wyatt was respectful toward me, as if I were still his alpha, but he suddenly had a sharp edge to his voice. He reached for her, but drew his hands back. "Rest now. We can talk later."

I wasn't sure how I felt about taking care of a strange fae girl who had been beaten and left to die in the forest, but I could see Wyatt's resolution. He wouldn't go anywhere until we helped her.

"We should find Keeran," I said, pushing up. "He might still have some healing herbs that can help her."

With the girl in his arms, Wyatt stood.

Her head rested on his shoulder and she looked up at him with her brilliant blue eyes. "I-I'm Farrah," she answered, her tone still weak, as if she would faint at any moment. "What's your name?"

"I'm Wyatt, and this is Luana." Wyatt jerked his chin toward me.

The corners of her lips curled up. "Thank you," she whispered. Then she closed her eyes and her head dropped back.

KEERAN HELD HIS TORCH HIGH. "WHAT HAPPENED? WHO is that?"

We met him halfway back. Wyatt and I explained how we had found her and showed him her wounds. Keeran seemed unsure about the fae girl, but he didn't hesitate in passing the torch to me and leaning over her to assess her injuries. To make things easier, I turned the torch into a fire and set up a crude camp, even though this spot wasn't the best, while Wyatt laid Farrah down on the bedroll and Keeran applied that healing herb to her wounds.

"Will she be all right?" Wyatt brushed the fae girl's hair back. If Farrah had been a werewolf, I would have guessed she was Wyatt's age, maybe a year or two younger, but as far as I knew, fae aged differently from us.

"I don't know." Keeran ripped some of her dress around her stomach, where a big gash ran through her side, caked with silver blood. "She has some nasty cuts and I don't know how fast fae heal."

I hoped she not only healed fast, but she healed correctly. We had no idea what had been done to her, if there was poison in her system, or even if she was going to react to Keeran's herbs and magic.

A long time passed while Farrah slept, Keeran treated her injures, and Wyatt watched over her. Bored and anxious, I wolfed up and went out for a quick run around the perimeter. This way, I burned some of my pent up energy and surveyed the surrounding areas, making sure whoever attacked Farrah wasn't prowling in the dark, waiting for an opportunity to attack.

But other than small animals and insects, I found nothing.

When I got back to camp, Farrah was still sleeping, Wyatt still hovered over her, and Keeran had spread out our dinner —bread, cheese, fruit, and muffins we had gotten from the Wildthorn coven before leaving this morning.

I sat beside him and picked up an apple. "How is she?"

He glanced to his patient across the fire. "Her pulse is strong and her wounds seemed to be responding to my herbs and magic."

"She didn't wake up yet?"

Keeran shook his head. "No, and if her blood loss and the extent of her injuries is any indication, she won't for a while."

What did that even mean? That she could stay like that for days? And we would just sit here with her? Meanwhile, Isalia was destroying my pack.

No, we had to find a way of waking her up.

I stood, intent on shaking her awake if I needed to.

I jumped back when Farrah sat up with a gasp. Eyes wide, she glanced around and scooted away, as if afraid of us.

My frustration and bitchy side faded away and a protective feeling washed over me, as if she were a wolf from my pack.

"It's okay." I crouched down and reached for her. "It's us, remember? Luana and Wyatt. We helped you down from the tree."

Her eyes first landed on me, then on Wyatt. She let out a shaky breath, but she stopped fighting. Whatever had happened to this girl hadn't been pretty. She tensed all over again when Keeran appeared by my side. "Who is he?"

"This is our friend, Keeran." I gestured to her legs, where patches of the herb could be seen. "He's treating your wounds."

The girl frowned at Keeran. "What are you?"

"A warlock," Keeran said, his voice proud. And I was proud of him for not wanting to hide anymore.

"I thought warlocks didn't exist," she said.

"I thought so too," Keeran muttered.

"What about you too?" Farrah looked to Wyatt and me. "What are you?"

"We're werewolves," Wyatt said.

Farrah pulled her legs closer and embraced her arms over her knees, brushing the herbs spread covering her skin. "Werewolves and fae are enemies."

"That might have been true once, but things are changing." Well, that wasn't as true as I hoped since Isalia had taken over the Dark Vale pack, but soon it would be. It had to. I rested my hand on hers. "There are people who are trying to bring peace among all supernaturals. Werewolves, vampires, witches, warlocks, fae ... all of them. And we are helping them."

"That's ..." Her shoulders relaxed a little. "That's nice."

"How are you feeling?" Keeran asked. His eyes darted from wound to wound, checking on them.

Farrah closed her eyes for a second. "A little lightheaded. Queasy. Hurt. And weak."

"What happened to you?" Wyatt asked.

Farrah's bright sapphire blue eyes gained an extra gleam as they filled with tears. "The Bonecrown witches found me in the woods and captured me. They planned on using me as a blood sacrifice, but I'm not sure what happened. Instead, they beat me up and hung me there to rot and die."

A chill ran down my spine. The Bonecrown witches had done this to her? Were they that evil?

Wyatt turned his hard gaze to me. "I do not like these Bonecrown witches."

Me neither. But it wasn't like we had a choice. If we wanted to find Keeran's mother and the warlock coven, we had to talk to them. Hopefully, they were more civilized than they seemed.

"Where is your family?" I asked, because certainly she couldn't be alone.

"My parents were murdered by the Bonecrown coven long ago. There used to be a fae community in these woods, but there are only a handful around now due to the coven's magic."

"Why didn't you leave?" Wyatt asked. Once more the hard tone of his voice didn't escape me. It was like he was hurting with Farrah.

"I can't." A tear rolled down Farrah's beautiful face. "The remaining fae and I have some sort of spell keeping us here, like a leash the witches put on us. Occasionally, they play hide-and-seek with us. But when they find us, they take us away." Farrah suppressed a sob. "Last night was my turn."

She had been hanging from the damn tree since last night? I was surprised she didn't die.

But I was glad too. I had had enough of death.

A plan formed in my mind.

"You're okay now." I patted her hand. "You're safe with us." I gestured to the towel spread behind us and the food on it. "Eat something, then try to sleep again. I'm sure you'll feel better tomorrow."

I stood and went back to my previous spot on the other side of the fire. Keeran sat down beside me and reached for a slice of bread. "If she was taken by the Bonecrown coven, she might know exactly where it is."

Wyatt's eyes met mine. He had heard Keeran.

"I know," I said. "I thought of that. But right now, let her rest."

OF COURSE, WYATT ARGUED WITH ME ABOUT FARRAH, BUT only after she was deep asleep.

"Do you have any idea how scared she is? She won't want to go back!"

One, I was still surprised by his sudden change. From the pup who followed me around and loved a good pat on the head, to a short-temper, overprotective wolf. Although I liked most of this change, I didn't like that he was directing it at me.

"Don't you know me?" I asked him. "I won't put her in danger. You'll see."

He argued some more, but finally, he quieted down and went to sleep. Because we were so close to the witches, I didn't trust having all of us sleep without a lookout, so the three of us took turns during the night.

To be honest, I half expected something to happen. More fae would find us, or the witches would attack us, but the night was oddly quiet.

In the early morning, Farrah woke up as I toasted some bread over the bonfire. "Want some?"

She scooted closer to the fire, seating between Wyatt and me. "Yes, please."

I handed her the warm, crunchy bread and put another one on the end of my stick. "Did you sleep well?"

"I think so." She bit down on her bread.

I glanced to Wyatt and Keeran. They didn't know my plan, and by the moon, I hoped I was right. "So, Farrah, we need to get to the Bonecrown coven."

The girl stilled, her sapphire blue eyes growing in size. "W-why?"

"We're hoping they can help us find someone," Keeran said simply. He picked at the muffin on his lap.

"But ... they are evil," Farrah whispered.

"We know," I assured her. "But we still need to talk to them." And here came the bit she wouldn't like. "Would you mind showing us where their coven is?"

The bread fell from Farrah's hands. "No. No, I can't. I have to stay far from them or they'll find me again. I can't go back there. If they find me—"

I put my hand on her leg. "It's okay. I understand, I truly do, but like I said, we really need to talk to them." Even if the thought of facing such evil witches brought a sudden sickness to my stomach. "That's why I'm ready to offer you a deal."

"W-what do you mean?"

"You said the Bonecrown witches put a spell on you to keep you from leaving." I took my bread out of the fire. "What if we can break that spell?"

"Can you?" Hope was smeared all over her words.

"To be honest, I don't know if Keeran can do it." Beside me, Keeran frowned. I didn't like ambushing him like this, but telling him about this beforehand wouldn't have changed anything. "But I'm sure he would be willing to try."

His dark eyes met mine, a harsh glint in them.

"And ... what do I have to do in return?" she asked, though I was sure she knew what I would ask.

"I want you to guide us to the Bonecrown coven," I said.

"Luana," Wyatt hissed, in a low voice, probably only I heard it.

Farrah shook her head and her arms started trembling. "I can't. I'm sorry ... even for my freedom. I can't."

"It's okay, Farrah," Wyatt said, his tone softer for her. "You don't have to do it."

"I'm sorry, Farrah," I said. "I wouldn't be asking if it wasn't important. But you're right. It's too dangerous." I didn't want to push the girl. She was young and had gone through something traumatic. I didn't want to add more damage to her already grim experience.

We all fell silent.

"But you're all leaving?" Farrah asked. She glanced at each of us, a worried knot in between her brows. "You're all going to pack up and leave and try to find the Bonecrown coven now?"

Keeran nodded. "That's the idea."

Farrah looked down at her curled hands. "What if I can get you close to it, like to the border of their territory, and tell you how to go the rest of the way? Would that work?" She lifted her head, her eyes finding Keeran's. "Would you still try to break their spell and set me free?"

Keeran exchanged a glance with me. Why was he silently asking what to do when he probably knew my answer? If he wasn't going to say it, I would. "Of course," I answered.

Keeran shot to his feet. "Luana, can I talk to you?"

I frowned. "Sure." I followed him through the trees, going several feet away from our camp. He halted and spun to face me, his dark eyes serious. "What is it? Don't tell me you aren't willing to try it."

"That's not it," he said, his tone bitter. "It's just that—" He pressed his lips tight.

I reached for him and rested my hand on his arm. "Keeran, it's me, Luana, your friend. You can tell me anything."

He let out a long sigh. "I told you I don't have good control of my magic yet. I even told you I lost it a few days ago and almost killed a witch. What if it happens again? What if I lose control and hurt her?"

I squeezed his arm, suddenly aware of the muscles of his biceps. Frowning, I dropped my hand and cleared my throat. "I believe in you. This situation is different. Giselle and the other witches were trying to hurt you. You lost your temper. Totally understandable. This time, it'll be different. No one is forcing you." I gave him a small smile, because well, I knew I irritated him sometimes. But I wouldn't today. I would make sure of that. "You might not be able to break the spell, but you won't hurt her. I'm sure of it."

The glint in his eyes softened and he took a long breath. "All right. Let's try this."

FARRAH LAY DOWN ON THE BEDROLL, AND WE ALL SAT AROUND her. Keeran closed his eyes and hovered his outstretched hands over her long, lean body, trying to find any trace of magic.

After a few minutes, he stopped, his hands over her ankles. "It's like a shackle," he said.

"A leash," Farrah whispered. She had said it felt like a leash sometimes. "Do you think you can break it?"

Again, Keeran glanced at me. "I'm going to try."

Keeran closed his eyes again and focused. His hands shone red and he worked his magic. Farrah pressed her lips together.

My brows curled down. "Does it hurt?"

"Not really," she said, her voice breaking. Sign that it was hurting. "I can feel it. The leash being stretched."

Keeran's hand glowed brighter. Farrah let out a yelp.

"Keeran, you might want to stop," I said, afraid he was going to end up hurting her, and if he did, he would never forgive himself.

"No!" Farrah stared at me, her eyes wide. "Keep going. I can feel it. It's tugging at me. Keep pulling it. It'll break."

Keeran spied at her. "Are you sure?"

"Yes!" she barked.

Shaking his head, Keeran shut his eyes again. His hands were now almost as bright as the sun. Farrah gritted her teeth, her heartbeat skyrocketed.

If this didn't end soon, I would—

"Done!" Keeran announced. Hands back to normal, he sat back and stared at Farrah.

Even breathing hard, Farrah jumped up and gave a twirl. Her silver hair glowed in the sunlight and thanks to Keeran's healing, her skin had gained a little color. Her dress was still ripped and smeared with her silver blood, but her wide smile and the glint in her eyes told us she was happy. "I can feel it. It's like the leash was ripped, like the weight that held me back is gone." Keeran stood and she threw herself at him, squeezing his shoulders. "Thank you." She stepped back and smiled at me. "Thank you. To all of you." Her eyes lingered on Wyatt for a moment longer. "And thank you for saving me in the first place."

Wyatt's cheeks flushed slightly. "No worries."

"Farrah," I called her. "I hate to spoil your mood, but we really need to get going. If you can, please, show us the way to the Bonecrown coven."

Farrah's smile died and she took in a long breath. "Come with me."

LUANA, WYATT, AND I FOLLOWED FARRAH THROUGH THE woods. At some point, the trees grew closer together, their crowns thicker, making the forest dark for this time of the morning.

I didn't like it.

Finally, after almost an hour of walking, Farrah halted beside a rocky hill forming the base of a mountain. "It's through here." Farrah pointed ahead, past the rocky hill. "Go north. You'll find a white stone path. Don't worry about following the path. They will find you before you arrive at the end." She hugged herself.

"Thank you, Farrah," I said.

"No worries." The girl took a step back, as if she couldn't wait to run away from here. And now that she was free, I bet she would.

"Luana," Wyatt called me. "I want to stay with Farrah."

Luana blinked at him. "What?"

He glanced to the rocky hill beside us. "I really don't like the sound of these witches. I would rather stay with Farrah."

"But …" Luana looked at Farrah. "Aren't you leaving?"

The girl shrugged. "I want to. I will. But I have nowhere to go."

"We'll go to the last town, get a motel room, and wait for you," Wyatt said.

I could see the wheels inside Luana's head working. On one hand, she liked the idea of keeping Wyatt away from the dark witches. What if they turned on Luana and me the moment we stepped onto the path? Wyatt was better off not with us. On the other hand, the idea of a teenager alone in such dangerous woods with a teenage fae, who was still slightly hurt, also wasn't appealing.

Trying to help, I said, in a low voice, lest I angered her too, "That's not a bad idea."

Luana glared at me. Then, she let out a sigh and said, "Okay, but you two should stay together and get out of the woods. Avoid other supernaturals. If anything happens, get to the Silverblood coven or DuMoir Castle and ask for help. Got it?"

Wyatt puffed his chest. "Yes!"

Farrah nodded.

Before Luana could change her mind, I tugged at the sleeve of her shirt. "Let's go."

Luana glanced at Farrah and Wyatt one more time, as if she had a thousand things to say to them, then she went with me.

The moment we crossed into Bonecrown territory, the sky darkened more. I picked up a branch from the ground and lit a fire on its tip. I handed the torch to Luana, then did it again for myself.

We found the path. Smooth white stones led up the mountainside. However, what littered the ground beside the stones brought a cold chill to my spine.

Bones. Lots and lots of bones.

"I really don't like this place," Luana muttered as we started up the path.

A new feeling crawled from the depths of my chest and seized my breath. I grabbed her wrist and pulled her close. "Just ... stay close. If anything happens, we run, okay?"

Frowning, Luana jerked her hand free. "I can take care of myself." She marched ahead of me.

"I know that." I caught up with her, matching her strides. Honestly, with her shorter legs, did she really think I would stay behind? "I'm not saying that because I don't think you can fight—"

She halted and faced me. "It sure seemed that way."

I wasn't sure why she was on the defensive. Maybe because she had lost to a crazy she-wolf? Even if the crazy she-wolf cheated, I bet Luana thought she should have won and ensured the safety of her pack. And because of that, her temper shot up easily.

I shook my head. "That was not what I meant."

Luana crossed her arms, as if she could contain her temper. "Then what is it?"

My eyes locked on hers, and despite myself, I took a step closer. "I know you can fight and defend yourself, if you need to." A new feeling grew in my chest, making it hard to breathe. "I don't know how to explain it. I know you're a freaking badass, believe me, but I want you to stay close to me. So I can help you and protect, yes, but mostly because I care—"

I shut my mouth, my eyes going wide. Luana stared at me,

caught by surprise. Truth be told, I was surprised too. I had felt like this for a couple of days now, but I hadn't acknowledged it. Or at least, I had tried not to. I ran a hand through my messy hair. But why would it be so bad to acknowledge it? For the first time in my life, I liked someone. I didn't want it to go away.

"Curse this shit ... yes, I care about you and I would rather not see you hurt ever again."

Luana didn't even blink as she stared at me, and for a moment, I was afraid she had stopped breathing too.

Shit, had I scared her? I mean, I was scared too. After all I went through with females, it felt dangerous to allow myself to feel anything else other than wariness for them, but it was the truth. I couldn't deny it anymore. I couldn't hide it.

But Luana didn't seem ready for it.

Shit, what if telling her I cared about her had spoiled our friendship? Was there a spell to go back in time a couple of minutes? I could try to create one. Then I could go back and keep my mouth shut.

I opened my mouth to spit out some lie about it all being a joke, but Luana's hand caught my eye. Slowly, she raised her arm in front of her, her hand close to her body, and drew a small circle with her finger.

Understanding dawn on me.

We were surrounded by the Bonecrown coven.

"Shit," I muttered.

The witches stepped out from their hiding places, stepping over the bones littering the ground as if they were walking over pebbles. Wearing long, black gowns and dark makeup that covered most of their faces, the ten witches raised their hands.

"We don't like trespassers," one of them hissed.

"And you two are trespassers," another one said, a happy tone in her voice.

"We don't want to fight," I said. Ten against two was a bit unfair.

"Too late for that." A witch threw a black bolt at me.

Hastily, I created a shield in front of Luana and me, but I hadn't had time to channel my magic properly and the shield broke upon contact. Beside me, Luana shifted into wolf form. The pieces of her ripped clothes fell to the ground.

A witch hurled black rays toward Luana. She ran around them, hiding from the rays, but getting closer to attack.

Distracted by Luana, I almost missed the bolt directed at me. I whirled around just in time, and it zipped by my face.

These cursed witches weren't kidding.

I channeled my magic. A red bolt appeared in my hands, but by the time I threw it, several other black bolts made their way to me. Coming from all sides, I had nowhere to go. The bolts hit me, sending a small electrical charge down my body.

Breathing hard, I fell on my knees.

This fight wasn't freaking over yet.

I gathered my hands to cast another bolt. A thick, black rope appeared around my wrists. Enraged, I channeled my magic, but it only tickled under my skin, doing nothing else.

"Don't bother," a witch said. "This rope neutralizes your magic."

To my side, Luana was back in her human form, her arms tied behind her back too. A witch pointed her finger at Luana, and using magic, lifted Luana to her feet.

I knew she didn't care about being naked in front of people, but I averted my gaze. From the corner of my eyes, I saw as another witch approached Luana. I jerked against my rope, but they only tightened and somehow pulled me straighter. I couldn't move.

"Don't fight it," a witch said. "The more you fight it, the hard it'll be to move."

"But—" I glanced at Luana. The witch who had gone to her hung a cloak across her shoulders, hiding Luana's naked body from view. I let out a relieved breath. For a moment, I thought she would hurt Luana.

"Now," one of them said. "Come with us."

When they moved, I moved.

But Luana refused to go.

The witch raised her hand and curled her fingers. Luana grunted as she was pushed forward by magic. "Like I said, don't fight it or you'll regret it."

"Luana," I said low, sure only she would hear me with her enhanced hearing. "Don't fight it, please. Besides, we need them to talk to us."

She shot me a glare, but let it go.

The witches guided us up the path. The rest of the way was uneventful, though rather disturbing. Bones, darkness, and even a little hint of mist surrounded us.

After half a mile up the mountain, the path opened to a plateau where dozens of houses sat clustered together, and beyond them, a small black castle. The witches took us through the main road toward the castle. More witches gathered to watch and snicker at us, as if we were cattle on parade.

There were no men among them.

I shuddered, remembering the barbaric ways of the Silverblood coven. If they had been evil when it came to men, how terrible would the witches of the Bonecrown be? I honestly hoped I never found out.

Once inside the castle, we crossed a small, dark foyer and

an archway into what looked like the throne room: a narrow room with a black stone floor and at the end a large throne made of bones.

The witch sitting on the throne rose, and her voluminous black gown spilled to the floor. Her hair was also black, and like the others, she had dark makeup smeared all over her face. A crown made of bones rested atop of her head.

"My oh my, it's not every day we have visitors," she said. Her shrill voice grated my ears. "Myra, who do we have here?"

The ringleader stepped forward and lowered her head. "We caught them sneaking up the path, my queen. We do not know their names, only that one is a warlock and the other is a werewolf."

The queen approached us, a crazed glint in her dark eyes. "I'm Corvina, the witch queen of the Bonecrown coven. Who are you?"

I faced the queen. "I'm Keeran, a warlock from the Silverblood coven, and this is—"

"I've heard of you." Corvina narrowed her eyes. "Their first warlock. The Silverblood witch queen welcomes you, but the rest of the witches don't." My story was so common now that even these evil witches who lived days away from us knew about me? Freaking great. "What brings you here, Keeran?"

I shifted my weight. "I'm looking for my mother. My last clue led me here."

"Your mother?"

"Yes. Her name is Acalla."

A hiss echoed through the throne room before it became eerily silent. I glanced around. All the witches had their gazes on the floor and their shoulders tense, as if they were afraid. Of what? Of whom? My mother?

Corvina's eyes rounded for a moment when I mentioned my mother's name, but she quickly wiped that surprised expression from her face. "I'll tell you all I know, but I want something in exchange."

My throat went dry. "What?"

A half grin stretched over her pale lips. "A blood sacrifice."

I knew it. That was what the Wildthorn queen had warned us about. And yet, I didn't know how to solve this problem. "A blood sacrifice. What do you mean? Do you need a drop of blood?" I tugged at my wrists, but they were still bound. "If it's just that, you can have mine."

A growl rose from Luana's throat.

Corvina shook her head. "No, not yours."

"I'll do it," Luana said through gritted teeth.

Corvina turned her wicked smile to her. The ropes around Luana's wrists disappeared.

"Luana, no," I called out, but she didn't hesitate.

Luana shifted one of her hands into a claw and sliced her other palm open. Myra quickly brought a rusty chalice and put it under Luana's hand. The blood dripped into the chalice and then I felt it. A thick, heavy magic, almost suffocating, spreading from the chalice to the rest of the room. The witches threw their heads back and moaned, as if the blood was feeding them, giving them strength. Was that how they kept their powers? With blood from others?

Corvina licked her lips as if she could taste Luana's blood. "My oh my, you're a powerful little pup."

The queen extended her hands forward, as if calling for the magic. I felt it when more power left the chalice and went to the witches, when more blood seeped from Luana's cut.

Even though she was a powerful wolf, the cursed witches were taking too much, and Luana swayed as she grew weak.

I hooked my arm around her waist, pulling her to me. Her head lolled back on my shoulder. "That's enough!" I cried. "Stop this."

I couldn't read the dark glint in Corvina's eyes as she glanced from me to Luana and back to me. But finally, she lowered her arms and the heavy power dissipated from the room like invisible smoke.

The moment the magic let go of Luana, she began to heal and her wound stopped bleeding.

Corvina looked at Luana as if she was her next meal. "That was delicious."

My stomach turned with nausea and disgust. I looked down at Luana. She looked paler than usual. These freaking witches had taken too much of her blood. "Are you okay?"

Groaning, she pushed away from me. "I'll be fine," she muttered.

I felt like helping her to a seat and watching over her, or healing her even though her wound was almost closed now, but I knew she wouldn't like if I fussed over her, especially not in front of an audience.

But later I was going to yell at her for doing something so stupid for me. That foolish warm feeling was back, along with pride and respect.

I pushed my feelings away and focused on the dark witch in front of me. I turned my enraged stare to the queen. "So, your turn now. Tell me about my mother."

Corvina's face lost its amused gleam. She let out a long breath and gestured to her throne at her back. "Follow me."

10

CORVINA MOVED HER HAND UP, AS IF SHOOING A FLY, AND THE tall wall behind her throne parted in two and retreated to the sides as if it was being carried by wheels, revealing a round room with the same black stone floor and cold walls. But the prominent thing was the black cauldron in the center. At least four feet wide and as tall as my waist, the freaking thing billowed dark smoke that twirled up to the round ceiling, gathering and dancing there.

Luana and I halted a good ways from the cauldron, but Corvina beckoned us forward. "Come see," she said. Wary, Luana and I approached the cauldron, our eyes on the rising smoke. "Watch."

The queen reached for the smoke. It broke apart and stopping rising. Instead, it formed a thin sheet atop the cauldron's mouth, parallel to the floor.

Smoke pillars as tall as my hand rose from that sheet. Slowly, they took shape.

"People," I whispered, my eyes transfixed on the small hooded figures.

"Warlocks, actually," Corvina said. "Long ago, warlocks ruled our world." As she spoke, the shadows moved like they were action figures. "But soon female witches outnumbered them." Shadowy bodies in gowns appeared around the warlocks. "And wiped them out almost to extinction." Only one hooded figure remained at the smoke stage. "One warlock was particularly strong. Evil, but powerful." The warlock doubled in size, and more details were visible: his long hair, his beard, and the intricacy of his clothes underneath his open cloak. "Known as the Warlock Lord, Soren wanted to take his warlocks and fight back against the witches, but outnumbered, he had no hope but to hide and continue to produce heirs that would join his cause."

That name again. "Who is Soren?"

"I'll get to that. Watch." The warlock was surrounded by witches half his size, holding babies in their arms. "Though he tried and tried, his heirs either were born without magic or they died soon after birth of natural causes." The witches and the babies disappeared, melting away on the smoke stage, and a person a head shorter than the warlock appeared by his side—a witch in a fluffy dress and billowing hair. "Until he met Acalla." I sucked in a sharp breath. "Though she wasn't her coven's queen, she was known as one of the most powerful witches in the land. Soren stole her from the Silverblood coven. With her, he was able to succeed and he fathered a powerful warlock."

I took a step back. "What?"

Before I could process what she was saying, Corvina went on. "But the plan backfired." A baby appeared in the witch's arm. "When this little warlock was born, a prophecy was created." The baby jumped from the witch's arms and started growing and growing, turning into a tall man with a long cloak. "The prophecy stated that Soren's son would become the most powerful warlock in existence, and he would overthrow his father's reign."

On the stage, the young warlock raised his arm toward Soren, who grasped at invisible hands at his throat and jerked as he was lifted in the air. "Fearing his son's power and greedily wishing to keep the throne for himself, Soren tried to kill him, but Acalla whisked him away." The young warlock disappeared in a whirlwind that settled in the witch's arms, once more carrying a baby. She ran as Soren chased after her. "She hid her son in the Silverblood coven as a human, then afraid of leading Soren directly to him, she fled." The woman left the baby on the smoky ground, and crying, she ran away. "First to the Wildthorn coven, but Soren found her there. Then she came here, but he found her here too. We helped her escape, but we don't know where she went next. The only thing we know is that Soren has been hunting her ever since." The baby and the witch faded into smoke. "And while he hunts for her, he fights other witches." Thin pillars sprouted from the shadowy stage, and figures with long dresses appeared in front of them, their arms bound around a pillar. "He kills them the moment he gets his hands on them." Smoke billowed around the witches, consuming them like fire." Then the pillars, the witches, and the fire evaporated into the air. The warlock stood tall and alone on the stage. "He stops at nothing."

I could have sworn the warlock smiled before melting away into the stage. A moment later, the stage crumbled and disappeared inside the cauldron. Another second ticked and the cauldron returned to spewing dark smoke that shot straight to the ceiling.

My mind, still ensnared by the little play that I had witnessed, was having problems catching up with all Corvina had revealed.

But Luana's sharp intellect and big mouth didn't need a moment. "Are you saying ... Soren is alive? He is Keeran's father? And Keeran is the one from the prophecy?"

"Correct," Corvina said.

I shook my head. Until a few days ago, I didn't have a mother or a father, and I could barely control my powers. Now, I was the son of a powerful witch and a terrifying warlock, and there was a freaking prophecy about me that said I had to kill my father.

No, this was too much.

I took another step back. "This doesn't make sense."

Luana turned to me. "Keeran ..."

"I know it's a lot to take in," Corvina said. "But it's the truth."

I thought I would find answers here, but now there were more questions in my head. Why did my mother drop me off at the Silverblood coven as a human? Didn't she know I was going suffer as a slave? Why didn't my magic manifest earlier? Did she do something? Where could she have gone? And hadn't Corvina said Soren was in hiding? How was he searching for my mother *and* hiding? Who the hell came up with this ridiculous prophecy? Me, the most powerful warlock in the world? The witch queen of the Bonecrown coven was crazy. Freaking mad. That was the only explanation for this absurd story.

A knot appeared between Luana's brows. "Let's say this is

all true ... you said Soren is in hiding. How will Keeran find him and fulfill the prophecy?"

I stared at Luana. "You're not buying this, are you?"

"He's not hiding anymore," Corvina said, ignoring me. "After a few years in hiding, Soren realized he was strong enough that he didn't need to hide. He built a castle called the Dark Witch Manor not too far from here, and to this day he still fights witches, except the few ones who serve in his army, and he still searches for your mother, Keeran. He's sure that if he finds her, he'll find you too. And he will kill you."

I flinched. "This is crazy."

Corvina took a step closer. Her face was devoid of all the wickedness I had seen before. She stared at me with serious, meaningful eyes. "Keeran, listen to me. I know this is a lot to take in, but it's the truth. I want you to think and process it all, but I have one more thing to say before I leave you alone."

More? I took in a sharp breath and braced myself. "What?"

"You must go after your father and kill him first." Her tone was loud, resolute, as if she was delivering another prophecy. "You need to become the Warlock Lord, the ruler of the Dark Witch Manor. That is the only way to stop Soren and put an end to his witch hunt and every other terrible thing he does."

I shook my head. "I'm not a killer. I only kill when I really need to."

Corvina's hand curled into fists. She was getting irritated with me. "You *have* to kill him."

Luana put her hand on her hip. "So what? You suggest we just march into his castle and kill him? It wouldn't be that easy."

"Luana!" I almost shouted. Why was she feeding the ideas

of this mad witch? "I'm not doing anything like that. The only thing I'm interested in is finding my mother."

"We might not know where your mother is," Corvina said. "But I do know this: She's hiding from Soren. Kill him and she'll come out of hiding."

11

I DIDN'T LIKE HOW DISTURBED KEERAN LOOKED. THE FURROW between his brows didn't leave his face, and he didn't say a word as Corvina and Myra took us through the castle, out to the back garden, down a hidden path halfway down the mountain, and toward a nice, hidden manor nestled in a clearing beside a cliff.

We halted on the stone path before the porch steps. "This manor is right at the border of our territory, but we haven't used it in years. I'm not sure the state of things inside. Here are some things you might need." She gestured to Myra, who offered a black bag to us. Keeran didn't move, so I grabbed it from her and spied inside. It looked like clothes. She was giving us clothes? "Myra will come back later to stock your kitchen and check if everything is working. Let her know if you need anything."

"Thank you," I muttered, still shocked she would hand us a house and other necessities.

"Don't take this as a kindness from me," the queen said. "The witches of the Bonecrown coven aren't kind."

"Then why are you doing this?"

"What? Giving you a place to stay? Feeding you?" she asked. I nodded. She glanced to Keeran. "Because I expect you to come to your senses and realize you must kill Soren." If Keeran heard her, he pretended he didn't. "But you might need some time to prepare." She looked at me again. "So, use this place as your base, for now. If you have allies, call them. We promise to not attack any of your friends."

Which reminded me. "We do have friends to call."

After I wrote a quick note to be sent to Wyatt and Farrah and asked Myra to deliver it to them—without hurting them —the two witches left.

I was alone with a brooding Keeran.

Finally, he looked up and took in the manor, a spread out, two-story gray building with two round turrets at the corners, tall, narrow windows covered by dark curtains, and a wide stone porch. No plants or vegetation other than the tall grass from the clearing surrounding the place.

It looked somber and under the gray skies—here, it wasn't as dark as at the thick of the Bonecrown coven—it looked haunted.

"If we go in and use her house, she'll think I agreed to her plan," Keeran said, his voice low, cold.

"Regardless, we need a place to crash for now." I tugged on his arm. "Come on. Let's rest for now." I was dying for a shower. "We can worry about the rest later."

I didn't stop to explore the house. Pulling Keeran with me, I crossed the wooden-floored foyer and went up the wide, winding stairs to the second story, where we found a long corridor and several closed doors. I opened the first one and spied inside. A library. The next one revealed some kind of office. The third one was a walk-in closet with linens and towels —all dusty, I bet. At the fourth and fifth doors I found suites. Like the linens and towels, the furniture and the bedsheets looked like they needed a good cleaning, but I wouldn't bother with that now. I pushed Keeran inside one of the bedrooms.

He looked around the suite. Queen four-poster bed with gray sheets, wooden nightstands, tall dresser, an armoire, and a door leading to what looked like an outdated bathroom. Not too bad for an evil lair.

I stepped back into the corridor.

"Where are you going?" he asked.

What did he mean? "To the other bedroom." I pointed to the door across the corridor. "I'll take a shower and change. Be back in a few minutes."

Before he could protest about not wanting to stay here because of Corvina's expectations, I strolled inside my new bedroom and closed the door. Back pressed against the door's cold wood, I sighed.

Even I couldn't wrap my mind around everything Corvina had told us; I couldn't imagine what Keeran was going through. I almost went back to his room, to talk to him, to comfort him somehow, but he had barely processed anything. He needed time to let go of his shock and absorb the news, digest it, and figure out a path. Maybe the last step could wait until we talked, but for now, he could use some alone time.

Meanwhile, I took a shower. The pipes rang loudly as the water burst through them, and I wondered if it was clean since nobody had used them in so long, but I pushed those thoughts away and scrubbed myself clean anyway. Better than being covered in dirt and blood from the fight with the Bonecrown witches this morning.

All the while, thoughts of Keeran and his destiny fleeted through my mind. Poor Keeran. He had suddenly found out he was a warlock, and now he knew he was more than that. He was supposed to become the most important warlock there ever was. His father was evil and was hunting his mother so he could find Keeran and kill him.

Suddenly, my problems seemed to shrink in size. I had been wanting to rush through Keeran's mission so we could get back to my pack and defeat Isalia ASAP, but now I wasn't sure that was the most pressing issue. Of course, I still became sick each time I thought Isalia could be murdering my wolves, but I couldn't simply abandon Keeran. I had to at least see some of it through, or bring someone else he trusted in and leave him in good hands.

After the shower, I rummaged through the bag Myra had handed me. The first item I pulled out was a long black dress. I threw that aside, now convinced I wouldn't find anything useful. The second item was a man's shirt and pants—ancient ones, but still usable. Then, to my surprise, I found black leggings and a leather vest. The clothes didn't fit me perfectly, but again they were better than my dirty outfit.

With the men's shirt and pants in hand, I opened my door ready to raise my hand and knock on Keeran's door.

But the door was open.

"Keeran?" I called, stepping in. My steps faltered when I saw Keeran standing in front of the window, his gaze somewhere on the horizon. He was lost in his own mind.

My eyes locked on him. On his bare back and the droplets of water that still ran down from his damp hair and went around his shoulders and back, making his skin shine. His skin and his muscles. I didn't recall ever seeing Keeran without a shirt. If I had, it had been during battle or some other tense situation where my focus would be somewhere else.

But now? Now, there was only him and me, and he was totally unaware that I was gawking at his wide shoulders and back and the muscles under his skin. His pants sat low on his waist, and I suddenly wished he would turn so I could see the muscles lining his chest and stomach too. Did he have that V every female talked about? Did it go low into his pants and—

Eyes widening, I gasped and slapped my mouth.

Moon be damned, what the hell was I thinking?

At that, Keeran turned around. "Oh, Luana, I didn't see you."

And, confirming my suspicion, I got a full view of Keeran's chest and stomach. Yup, there were ripped muscles for miles and he did have the damn V.

My cheeks grew hot.

I threw him the shirt and averted my eyes. "That was in the bag Myra gave to us."

"Thanks." I didn't see as he caught the shirt and put it on. It was only when he stepped closer that I finally looked back at him. "I'm sorry for my bad mood. I'm still not sure what to think."

I sat down on the edge of the mattress and patted the spot beside me. "Want to talk about it?"

With a half grin, Keeran rolled his eyes, but took the seat. "I'm not sure. I don't even know where to start."

"We can talk about all of it. From the beginning, if you want."

He looked at me, his gaze meeting mine and holding it there. "I'm glad you're here with me." The tone of his voice ...

I cleared my throat. "So, tell me. What is bothering you the most?"

Keeran's eyes became two slits. "You know what? I don't want to talk about it."

He began to rise, but I reached up and closed my hand around his wrist. "Keeran, I'm your friend. You know that, right? Whatever is bothering you, you can tell me. If your thoughts are jumbled, we can talk through it until we straighten them out."

Keeran closed his eyes and lowered his head, his chin almost touching his chest. Then, when I thought he would break free of my grip and run away from this conversation, he sat back down and looked at me. "A quick list: My father is evil and hunting my mother and me, my mother is hiding to protect me, and I'm supposed to kill my father and become the Warlock Lord. Did I miss anything?"

I thought about it. "Nope. I think you got it all."

Groaning, Keeran brought the heel of his hands up and pressed them against his eyes. I dropped my hand from his arm. "All I wanted was to find my mother and more warlocks like me. That was all." He lowered his arms and stared straight ahead, to a blank spot on the wall across the room. "I don't want to kill anyone, especially not a man who is supposed to be my father, and I certainly don't want to be the Warlock Lord."

It dawned on me that now Keeran encountered himself in a situation similar to mine. His people were being ruled by an evil leader. Only when he took out that leader could he help his people, show them what peace meant.

This damn mission was taking way longer than planned. My heart tugged at the thought that the longer I stayed away from my pack, the longer it took me to reclaim my pack, the more chances Isalia had to kill the wolves, to make them suffer.

But I couldn't go back there alone. If I did, Isalia wouldn't let me go this time. She would kill me on sight. I needed help. I needed Keeran's help. But before he could help me, I had to help him.

"What is it that you want?" I asked. "If you could do anything, be anyone, what would you choose?"

He stared at me for a moment, thinking. "I don't know." I felt more than I saw as his soul deflated. He probably had never thought about that, and I was suddenly adding more troubling thoughts to his head. "I really don't know." A long breath escaped from his lips. "Right now, I would rather go back to the Silverblood coven. Or DuMoir Castle. There are less witches there."

"But you know you don't really fit there." I wasn't trying to be mean; I was trying to help him, to guide him to the right path. "Neither of us did. I know Drake and Thea are wonderful people, and they would forever put up with us, but their covens aren't our covens. We made friends for life, but staying with them isn't our ... destiny." I held my breath, afraid he would lash out at me because of that word.

Keeran groaned. "Do you believe that? In destiny? Do you think we have a fate? Do you think this cursed prophecy is mine?"

"I don't know," I whispered. As much as I liked to think we were destined to do great things, I had never stopped and considered it. So far, I had done what I felt was right.

"This is all so messed up."

"It's okay. You don't have to figure it all right now." I pushed up to my feet. "Come on. It's probably past lunchtime and I'm hungry. Let's see if we can find something to eat."

Myra must have come to the manor while we were taking showers, because the kitchen was stocked and the floors and counters were free of dust. We found some pasta and condiments for red sauce, so we whipped that up.

In silence, we sat down around the oval table beside the kitchen and ate. I could see Keeran's mind continued to work through our discoveries, but he was nowhere close to finding a solution.

I wanted to tell him about my thoughts; I just wasn't sure he was ready to hear them. Because, like Drake had stepped up to get control of DuMoir Castle, and Thea had chosen to be the witch queen of the Silverblood coven until Aurora was older, and I had to take back my pack to save them from a crazed alpha, I believed Keeran didn't have a choice here. He *had* to follow this calling, this prophecy, and confront his father. He had to reign over the warlocks so they stopped hunting witches and killing them, and finally the supernatural world could know peace.

Despite the strong feeling I had about this, Keeran wasn't ready to hear it.

So, I chose to be quiet, for now. When we were done eating and cleaning up, I suggested we go for a stroll outside, around the manor. The clearing and the cliff looked beautiful, and it would be nice to be outside and breathe in some fresh air.

Once more silence reigned as we walked through the tall grass. It was a comfortable silence though. It always had been with Keeran. I glanced at him, still stunned about how handsome he was and how I wanted to reach over and hug him and tell him everything would be all right. He had left his cloak behind, but even with his closed off expression and drooped shoulders, he looked every bit as impressive and powerful and striking.

Or was it just me? Was I the only who saw him that way?

We walked to the cliff and we skirted the edge, going down along the mountain, until it opened into a little stream flanked by roses of all colors. The sun filtered through the trees, making the water shine against my eyes and enhancing the colors of the roses. The water, the roses, the sweet scent of the flowers, and the vibrant green all around? It took my breath away.

What a piece of heaven right behind such a dark place.

Keeran crouched next to the red roses and picked one up. The rose shone in his hand as magic enveloped it. A moment later, the shine was gone, leaving behind a crystalized rose.

Turning to me, Keeran offered me the rose. "This way, it'll never rot." I froze, confused. Shocked. What was he doing? Why was he offering me a rose? When I didn't move, Keeran reached over with his other hand. He took my hand in his and placed the rose in my palm. "I know it's simple, but it means a lot."

"I ..." I stared at the rose, trying to grasp what he was trying to say. Earlier this morning, he said he cared about me, and now he was giving me a crystalized rose. Was this his way of telling me he liked me? "Thank you," I whispered, not sure what else I could say.

He ran a hand through his hair, then locked his eyes with mine. "I wanted ..." He paused, a frown marring his forehead. "I'm—"

I didn't know what overcame me. I stood on my tiptoes and leaned into him. I cupped his face as I brought my lips to his.

Only, I didn't kiss him.

Keeran stepped back, and I had to catch myself before I fell face-first on the ground.

Shame and embarrassed took hold of me. "Hm, that was—"

"Excuse me," Keeran said, before he spun around and darted toward the manor.

And I stood there, clutching the rose he had given me.

12

I PACED MY BEDROOM, MY HEAD MORE CONFUSED BY THE minute.

What the hell had I done? I had led Luana on and then cut her off.

My heart told me I had been a coward, but I couldn't do it for two strong reasons.

One, I had never kissed a woman before. What the Silverblood witches had me do when they abused me wasn't kissing. They had kissed me; I had never kissed them back. All the intimate contact I had in my entire life had been against my will. For the first time, I wanted to kiss someone and I wanted to touch her, but every time I closed my eyes, anticipating the moment, I saw those cursed witches taunting me and torturing me and abusing me. My stomach knotted, my breathing sped up, my heartbeat hurt. How could I kiss Luana like that?

And two ... because I was hiding a secret from her and I couldn't accept her affection until we had everything out in the open. This lie between us was killing me. I couldn't keep it from her anymore.

Not an hour after leaving Luana by the creek, I went looking for her. By now I thought she would be back at the manor, but I scoured every inch of the freaking place and couldn't find her. Was she still at the creek? By herself? Shit, I was really a jerk.

I dashed toward the last place I had seen her, but stopped short when I saw her on the edge of the cliff, looking down.

My heart stopped.

What in ...?

Desperation pushed my legs faster than they ever moved and I ran to her. I grabbed her hand and pulled her several feet from the cliff.

"What do you think you're doing?" I asked, my voice hitching a little.

She frowned. "Looking at the view."

I blinked. "W-what?"

Her eyes rounded. "You thought I was going to jump?" She stuffed her chest and lifted her chin. "I might be mortally embarrassed over your clear rejection, but I wouldn't kill myself. I thought you knew me better than that."

A long breath shuddered through my throat. Thank goodness, it wasn't as I first thought. But I then realized something. The panic that gripped me when I saw her at the edge of the cliff still had its clutches around me, even after the situation had been explained, not because I didn't understand what she had been doing, but because I was afraid of losing her. Now. Today. Tomorrow. In any situation. I couldn't lose her.

This feeling, this adoration, this want, this need—it was all for her. I liked her, even maybe more than that, and I couldn't lose her.

But I was about to.

"I didn't reject you," I said. Hands on her hips, Luana let out a huff. "I know it looks like that, but I didn't reject you." I took a step closer to her, hoping she wouldn't dart away. Not yet. "I told you before, I care about you."

She shook her head. "Stop, Keeran. I can't and I don't want to play games."

"This isn't a game." I took in a long, encouraging breath. It was now or never. "But I have something to tell you before I can prove to you how much I care about you."

Clearly annoyed—it was her way of shielding herself— Luana crossed her arms. "This should be good."

"You cheated too," I blurted out before I lost the courage. Luana looked at me as if I was talking another language. "I mean, you didn't cheat per se, but Drake and I were watching your fight with Ulric. Both of us noticed you weren't faring too well. At one point, Drake almost intervened and killed Ulric himself, but I stopped him. However, there at the end, Ulric had you. He was going to kill you. I couldn't just watch. I used my magic and sent an electric current through Ulric's body. He let go of you because of that, and you were able to recover and kill him first."

Slowly, Luana's eyes and lips rounded and her arms fell to her sides. "You ... No ... But I ..." She glanced around, as if searching for answers around the clearing, or down the cliff. "You're saying I became alpha because you helped me cheat?"

"I'm sorry." It was all I could say, and I knew it wasn't enough.

Luana pressed a hand over her stomach. "And here I was, feeling so righteous that I was the true alpha of the Dark Vale pack. That Isalia had cheated, taking my place." Her eyes filled with tears, and her lips curled down in what sounded like a snarl. "And I did the same."

I reached for her. "No, it's not your fault."

She took a step back, getting out of my range. I glanced to the cliff, afraid she would slip and fall. "Nevertheless, I'm not the alpha. I never was, not really. It was a lie." Her hands curled into fists. "Moon be damned, I was never a rightful alpha."

"Luana ..."

"I knew ... I knew I was never fit to be alpha. During my year in command, I thought I had been so damn lucky to have won, but I also thought I could do my best. I could try to be the best alpha my pack could have." She wrinkled her nose. "My pack. They aren't *my* pack anymore."

"That's not true."

"I don't know what to do anymore," she whispered.

"You can—"

Luana lifted her hand, her index finger up as a warning. "You shut the hell up. I don't want to talk to you." She took another step back. "Ever again."

Luana wolfed out. Her ripped clothes fell to the ground, and she dashed across the clearing.

"Luana!" I called out, knowing she could hear me.

A moment later, she disappeared down the path.

I WENT AFTER HER, BUT I SOON REALIZED SHE WAS TOO FAST for me. I would never catch up with her.

Hoping she just needed some time to cool off, I dragged my feet back to the flower patch. I picked up the crystalized rose she had dropped when she wolfed out. I wasn't sure what I had meant when I gave it to her. I just ... wanted to give something beautiful to her, something beautiful like her.

Holding on to the rose, I made my way back to the manor.

My mother, my father, the warlock coven, the prophecy, now Luana ... my thoughts were jumbled and trying to think through it all hurt. I had to do something to pass the time before I drowned inside my own head.

Since there was nothing else to do here, I might as well practice.

In the gloomy living room on the first floor, I cleared some space, pushing the outdated furniture to the side, and positioned myself in the middle of the open area. Closing my eyes, I channeled my magic and filled my veins with my power. I took in a deep breath and opened my eyes. A red bolt appeared in my open palm.

I wanted to control it. To make it bigger, to make it smaller, to bounce it in the air, to throw it at the wall and stop it at the last second, calling it back to me.

But the moment I focused and thought about the bolt becoming bigger, my magic flickered. The bolt crackled and sparkled. In three seconds, it was bigger than my chest. The bolt exploded in a million shiny sparks.

I cowered under my arms as the sparks flew around the living room. They singed the walls, broke the mirror by the entranced, burned a hole through the couch, and cracked a vase in the corner of the room.

It seemed I couldn't even practice magic.

Defeated, I plopped down on the couch, and with my elbows on my knees, dropped my head in my hands.

"What happened?"

I snapped my head up at the new voice. Wyatt and Farrah stood in the doorway, gawking at the ruined living room. "Oh, um, nothing." I pushed up. "I see you got Luana's message. Everything okay coming here? No problems with the Bonecrown witches?"

Farrah shuddered. "I didn't want to come, but Wyatt insisted that if Luana said it was safe, then it was."

"Speaking of Luana ..." Frowning, Wyatt inhaled deeply and looked around. "I can smell her scent, but it isn't recent. Where is she?"

I groaned as frustration came back full force. "About that ..." I told them what happened. Well, almost everything. I told them I confessed to Luana about having helped her win against Ulric and she ran off. "I'm hoping she's just cooling off somewhere."

Wyatt scoffed. "Cooling off? Don't you know Luana? She's a wolf, you idiot. She's going to do something stupid first that she'll regret, then afterward, she's going to cool down and hate herself." Shit, I hoped he was wrong. "How long has she been gone?"

I checked the grandfather clock along the wall. By a miracle, that thing had survived time and still worked. "About two hours, I think."

"Plenty of time to do something stupid," Wyatt said with a snarl.

Panic replaced the frustration and took hold of my chest, making it hard to breathe. "We should go after her."

13

THERE WAS NO THOUGHTS IN MY MIND AS I RAN DOWN THE
path, past the mountain, through the forest. No thoughts,
only a dark feeling. A dark anger.

On my wolf legs, I was fast, too fast for a human, and I
soon cleared miles between Keeran and me.

But once I allowed myself to slow down, the thoughts
were back.

I hadn't won against Ulric. Not honorably.

Because of Keeran, I had cheated, which didn't make me
much better than Isalia.

I stomped my paws on the ground, halting with a jerk. I
would rather have died than win by cheating. Drake and
Keeran should have let me die!

Then, this gigantic hole of shame wouldn't be eating at
my chest, suffocating me. Shame over cheating, shame over
thinking I could be a good alpha, shame over *wanting* to be
alpha, shame for exposing my feelings to the wrong person
and being rejected.

A low, painful howl scratched at my throat.

I was now a lone wolf, and as such, I pushed from my paws and went for a hunt. The thrill of the hunt would take my mind off the shameful things filling my chest and head, not to mention the sun would set soon and I would want a bite then.

I caught the scent of rabbits. I preferred hunting deer, but as it was, rabbits would make a decent meal too.

I slowed down and crouched behind a bush, silent as a dead wolf, so as not to scare the five rabbits munching on a bunch of clover a few feet from my hiding place. Poor things would never see me coming.

The littlest one hopped closer. It stopped, looked up, sniffed.

I doubted it could smell me, but just in case ...

I jumped from behind the bush and landed with two of my paws on the rabbits. My jaw closed around a third one. After a cracking sound, I dropped the rabbit from my mouth and advanced to the next two.

But I barely took a step when a new scent reached me.

When I looked up, my breath hitched as five men stepped out from behind the trees, spears in hand, their sharp blades pointed at me. It didn't take me two seconds to realize I had seen their features before: white or gray or silver hair, fair, smooth skin, delicate features, and slightly pointed ears.

Fae.

"This is the one?" one of the fae asked. They wore elegant but worn out white and silver armor from head to toes. "Are you sure?"

"Yes," another one said. "She was with the Bonecrown witches."

The first one jutted his spear toward me. "Shift back,

wolf." He spat the word as if it meant something evil. "Don't make this more difficult than it has to be. Shift!"

I snarled. I wasn't sure I could take on five grown fae, especially because I didn't know much about fae and their abilities, but I could run. I pushed on my hind legs, getting ready to dash away. Another five fae appeared behind me, their spears also aimed at me.

The group surrounded me.

Damn, now it would be hard to run.

If I knew what they wanted...

Reluctantly, I shifted into human form. A long, white cloak was thrown to me mid-shift. With the cloak secured around my shoulders, I stood tall and faced the fae. "What do you want?"

"Why did a filthy wolf enter the Bonecrown territory?"

"And came back alive."

"Which means, you're on their side."

"No reason to deny it."

"You're just as evil as they are."

The fae kept throwing accusations at me, as if I had been in league with the witches to kill them all. I frowned. Farrah had said the fae moved away from the witches, but a few like her had stayed behind because of the spell that kept them near the coven.

However, these fae ... they didn't seem lost and alone, like Farrah suggested. If anything, they seemed like soldiers on a hunt.

"Wait, wait ..." I pressed my eyes closed for a moment. "You think I'm working with the Bonecrown witches? That's ridiculous."

"Don't deny it," the one closest to me said. "You're working with them to kill us."

"Take her!" another one shouted.

I immediately started shifting, to fight my way out as a wolf, but one of the spears hit me in the back, sending a jolt of cold energy down my spine. A yelp erupted from my throat and my body shook violently, my muscles locking up and my teeth gritting. Dizzy, I fell on my knees.

"W-what is this?" I asked, trying to fight whatever was happening.

"You can't win, little wolf," one of the fae said. Arms hooked around me and hauled me up. "Move."

I blinked. If I tried to take a step, I would only falling on my face. "I can—"

The cold jolt came back. Maybe because it was the second time, it was stronger. I crumbled on all fours, groaning as my muscles spasmed with the jolt that ran through them.

The blade of the spear poked my back again, this time without its power. "Move or we'll keep zapping you."

Without much of a choice, I sucked in a deep breath, willing my vision to clear and my muscles to relax enough so I could move, and pushed up.

"Where are you taking me?" I asked, my throat hurting as my voice scratched it.

"No questions." The fae pushed his spear toward me, teasing me. "Just move."

The fae created a living wall around me as we started walking through the woods. With each step we took, a desperate feeling filled me. What would happen to me? What if the fae killed me? Nobody would ever know what happened to me, where my body was. I would never get a proper burial.

I knew Keeran was probably holed up inside the manor at the edge of the Bonecrown territory, but I couldn't just do nothing. Hoping someone would hear me, I lifted my chin up and let out a long howl.

The zap came from my shoulder this time. I practically fell over one of the fae, who held me up, but he pushed me away a second later.

I swear, this zapping thing would kill me soon. But if someone had heard my howl and knew where to find my body, it would have been worth it.

14

WE DIDN'T RUN THROUGH THE FOREST, BUT WE HIKED FAST, AS fast as our human legs could go. Knowing Luana's short temper, she had probably gone looking for trouble and now couldn't get out by herself.

The feeling surrounded me, pressing on me. This time, I was sure her trouble was big.

We hadn't marched down the mountain and through the trees for an hour when Wyatt announced, "I've picked up her scent again."

Good. That meant we were on the right path.

Then I heard it.

A thin, shrill howl.

My heart skipped a beat. I turned huge eyes to Wyatt. "Is that ...?"

His brows slammed down. "Yes, that's her."

We ran after the howl, Farrah a few steps behind, even though I was sure that with her fae heritage she was faster than me. I hated being the only human in the group.

Wyatt stopped near a clearing. The sun was setting and the shadows grew fast. I picked up a branch from the ground and lit its tip on fire. Then I pointed it down to whatever Wyatt was starting at.

Three dead rabbits.

"What happened here?" I asked, confused.

"It was her," Wyatt said. He pointed to small tracks. "There were more rabbits, but something stopped her and she couldn't get to them." He inhaled deeply. "This way."

He dashed out again and I scrambled to follow. Even if he wasn't wolfing out for my benefit, he was still fast. And Farrah still kept herself a few steps behind us.

A few minutes later, Wyatt stopped again. He put his hands to his lips and spied around a twisted tree trunk. I extinguished the fire of my improvised torch and dropped it before I crouched beside Wyatt and pushed aside a curtain of leaves.

I held in a gasp.

In the clearing a few yards from us was a camp full of fae. But the camp didn't look temporary. The huts looked crudely put together with fallen branches and small tree trunks, but they seemed to have been there for a while. There were wooden benches here and there, and tall wooden pillars hosting lit torches. In the center, the fire billowed high and powerful.

Fae fussed over something huddled beside the fire. When they stepped back, I saw her.

Luana.

She looked disoriented, if not hurt.

A white cloak covered her body.

About ten fae held spears and kept them pointed at her.

I turned to Farrah and she cowered before me. "You said

there weren't many fae around here, that they had left." I pointed to the clearing a few ways behind me. "How do you explain that?"

She looked down, her shoulders turning in some more. "I'm not welcome here," she muttered, her voice low. Afraid.

Wyatt joined us. "You weren't alone?"

Farrah looked at him, her blue eyes saddened. "I was kicked out, okay? I can't go back."

"What happened?" I pressed. "Why were you kicked out?"

She crossed her arms. "I don't want to talk about it."

I took a step back and stared at her. I knew next to nothing about fae, but I had heard they could be a treacherous bunch who lied left and right for their own benefit. Yesterday, we had rescued a lone fae, thinking she was alone and lost and sad, but she had lied to us. And now, confronted, she still didn't want to reveal anything to us.

"You aren't going to help us, are you?" She didn't answer. For the first time since we found her, Wyatt looked at her with disappointment written all over his face. I took another step back. "Let's go, Wyatt."

By my side, Wyatt wolfed out and I channeled my power. If we were going to attack, we better be prepared.

Without a clear plan, Wyatt and I barged into the clearing.

The fae noticed us approaching. A dozen of them stepped out from the crowd to meet us halfway. Wearing battered white and silver armor, the twelve fae aimed their sharp spears at us.

A tall male fae with long white hair stepped up to the sudden barrier and asked, "Who are you?"

"We don't want any trouble," I said, raising my hands in

peace. Underneath, I was already channeling my magic. "We're here for our friend. The werewolf."

"She's our prisoner," the fae said, his tone absolute.

Rage coursed through me. "Hand her over and let us go, or there will be trouble."

The male fae snorted, amused. "You don't stand a chance." He jerked his chin toward us and the soldiers advanced.

Wyatt let out a snarl and I cast a bolt. We were ready.

A fae pushed his spear toward me, but I jumped back and let my bolt fly. I sent a couple more. It hit them right away; they were enough to make the fae dizzy, but not to kill. All I wanted was to rescue Luana and not kill anyone.

I dodged their spears and threw bolts, taking a couple of fae down. By my side, Wyatt also evaded their attacks, but he couldn't do much without getting close.

A fae sneaked behind me and hit my back with the blade of the spear. Magic that felt like a powerful cold shock ran down my spine, and I fell on my knees, shaking all over. My magic slipped from my fingers.

What was that freaking spear?

Another fae came at me, his spear ready to hit me.

I called on my power as fast as I could, and with my magic, I took hold of his spear and the spears of other three fae. They fought against it, but with my temper rising, my power grew too, and I easily turned the spears on them and zapped them.

A yelp came from my side and I saw Wyatt trembling on the ground as a fae pushed his spear into the young wolf's side.

Worse than the yelp was Luana's scream. I spied around

the fallen fae. She too fought against her captors, but like us, she had been brought down by the cursed spears.

Pushing against the pain and dizziness, I stood and channeled my power.

The blade of a spear hit my shoulder. Another one pushed against my back. A third one pressed against my chest.

"Stop this," the leader said.

I shook my head. My magic felt unstable in my veins, but it was the only thing I had. "I can't. Until you let the three of us go, I can't."

I pulled my arm back, intent on throwing my magic at the leader.

A powerful icy jolt traveled down my body and I grunted, fighting the freaking pain.

"Stop!" someone boomed.

Black spots danced in the corner of my eyes, but I looked in its direction.

With her long hair dancing behind her as if she were underwater, Farrah walked into the clearing. At her presence, the fight stopped, but that allowed the fae to surround Wyatt and me. Now, if we dared breathe the wrong way, we would be hit again.

My vision cleared and I realized Farrah was shining. A white light surrounded her as she weaved through the fae.

The fae hissed as she walked past them, but the leader stood still, his icy blue eyes going from rage to sadness in two seconds. "You shouldn't be here."

"I know, Daleigh. I know. But these are my friends. I came to collect them."

Daleigh snorted. "You think I'll allow you to take them?"

Farrah held his gaze, her eyes softening too. "I don't want to fight," she whispered.

"Then don't."

Farrah let out a long sigh. "Let them go."

Daleigh's eyes narrowed. He looked from Luana, to Wyatt, to me, then back to Farrah. "I'll let them go. If you stay."

What was going on here? How did they know each other? And what had Farrah done that she wasn't welcomed, but the leader asked her to stay nonetheless?

She shook her head. "I can't ..."

"Farrah—"

"Enough chat." A fae pointed his spear to Farrah's chest. Wyatt let out a snarl. "Leave or join them. Your choice."

"Bracken!" Daleigh shouted. "I'm in command here."

"You're too soft when it comes to her." Bracken jerked the spear in her direction.

As if she were stroking a pet, Farrah reached forward and wrapped her hand around the spear's blade. Wyatt let out a loud yelp and I stopped breathing. The magic hit Farrah, but it didn't shock her. No, she called it in, letting it flow inside her like it was her magic. Her eyes shone white for a brief moment. Then, the magic rushed out of her, traveling through the spear and shocking its holder.

The male fae fell to the ground, jerking with the force of the hit.

"Let us go," Farrah whispered, a resolute tone to her words.

"But they were helping the Bonecrown witches," Daleigh said.

Farrah shook her head slightly. "They aren't on those witches' side. I guarantee it. You have it wrong. Now, please, let us go."

Daleigh held her stare for three heartbeats. "Back off," he ordered. "Let Farrah and her friends go."

It took them a second, but one by one, the fae lowered their weapons and stepped back.

Channeling my magic to give me strength, I rushed toward Luana. She had fought against the fae as we had—and she had been hit by the magic from the spear. That and whatever else they did to her before we got here had her weak.

I hooked my arm around her waist and pulled her to me. "Are you okay?"

"Let's just get out of here before they change their minds," she whispered. I knew she wasn't feeling great when she leaned against me and allowed me to half-drag her from there.

Farrah ushered Wyatt, Luana, and me along while she stood her ground, as if the moment she turned her back on them, they would change their minds and attack.

Thankfully, they didn't. But the whispers and hisses and strange words that sounded like curses echoed from the crowd as we marched away.

It felt like we were being pushed away from yet another group. Banished again, as if we didn't fit anywhere.

"Keep going," Farrah muttered once we exited the clearing. "Just keep going."

I stopped long enough to pick up a branch and light it as a torch as it was getting too dark to see. Well, at least for a warlock like me.

We walked for thirty minutes before Farrah finally relaxed. Suddenly halting, she put a hand over her heart and let out a long breath.

Wyatt shifted back into his human form and got dressed

while I helped Luana to a fallen branch. Then, I turned on the fae, my torch high. "What was that?"

Farrah shook her head vehemently, her eerie white hair swaying side to side. "I *really* don't want to talk about that."

"Farrah ..." Wyatt's tone was full of begging. Longing. She turned her eyes to him. "Tell us. Please."

Something in her cracked, because her shoulders slumped and she said, "Daleigh. He's the leader of that group ... and my brother."

That was a surprise.

"What happened?" Wyatt asked. "He kicked you out?"

"Also, you said there weren't many fae around here," I reminded her. "But we just saw a bunch of them."

"This is all I'm going to tell you: My brother and I don't have the best relationship," she said. "Yes, I was kicked out and I won't tell you why." She fixed those bright blue eyes on me and continued, "There aren't many fae around here. Daleigh and his people? That is nothing compared to the fae population, but they are back in our realm. Daleigh will join them soon, I think." She looked at the ground. "I hope."

Groaning, Luana pushed to her feet. She gripped the white cloak, keeping it around her body. "That is all great." Sarcasm dripped from her words. "But if you all will excuse me, I need to go now."

A sudden wave of rage surged through me. "And do what? Get caught by the fae again?"

She flinched. "I just ..." She didn't finish it. She turned and took a step away from us.

"Luana," Wyatt called.

I rushed forward and stepped in her way. "Okay, okay ... I'm sorry."

"Get out of my way." She lifted her hazel eyes to mine and I could see the hurt there as clear as day. "Please."

"No, I—"

"I don't care if you didn't win the fight against Ulric fair and square," Wyatt said, approaching us. "Isalia cheated too. Despite that, you two can't be compared. You're so much better than her. The pack will be better off in *your* hands, not hers."

"He has a point," I whispered.

Luana cut me a glare. I guess she was still mad at me. Well, I couldn't blame her for that.

"And this time, you can win for real." Wyatt looked at me. "Nobody will interfere; we promise you." I nodded in agreement. Although, when I remembered the last time—Ulric holding her down and about to kill her—I wasn't so sure. Could I really watch her die? "We'll just do some crowd control, but other than that, the main fight will be yours. And you can have your pack back with honor."

"To be honest, I don't know if I should be alpha," she confessed.

"What are you talking about?" Wyatt frowned. "You're much better than Isalia."

Luana raised a finger. "I agree with that, but I'm still not sure I'm the best one for the pack. Perhaps we can think of another wolf within our pack who can take her place. We'll assist him in defeating Isalia."

"But Luana—"

Wyatt's protests died on his lips and both Luana and he snapped their heads to the side. They had caught a sound.

I freaking hated when that happened.

"What is it?" I asked, feeling out of the loop without

having enhanced hearing. Beside us, Farrah was quiet, and I wondered if fae had a freakishly good hearing too.

Luana sniffed the air. "A wolf ..."

She and Wyatt stepped forward as a wolf limped past the trees and fell on the ground in front of us. I brought my torch closer to inspect it. Blood covered almost all of its brown fur.

The wolf was dying.

15

LUANA

I RECOGNIZED HER SCENT AND FORM INSTANTLY.

"Macy." I knelt down beside her, my hands hovering over her mangled body. I was afraid of touching her and making her hurt more. "W-what happened?"

Slowly, Macy shifted from her light brown wolf form to her slim human body. The wounds and blood were more visible and looked even worse in her tanned skin. Keeran shrugged off his cloak and covered her body with it.

"It was Isalia," she whispered. "She has gone mad." She coughed and blood slipped past her lips.

"Luana," Keeran called. "She's dying. If you want a chance for me to heal her, we need to move her to the manor *now*."

I could hear her weak heartbeat and her shallow breathing, but for some reason, Keeran's words made it more real. Another one of the Dark Vale wolves dying, and all because of Isalia.

Weight pressed against my chest, and I fought not to

break down under it. I gave Keeran a short nod. He reached for her, but Wyatt was faster. "I can do it."

Wyatt, though younger, was stronger than Keeran because of his wolf blood. Together, the five of us rushed to the manor. We invaded one of the empty, dusty bedrooms, and Wyatt deposited Macy on the bed. Keeran didn't waste time. He grabbed his herbs and sat down at the edge of the bed, ready to heal her.

But Macy slapped his hand away as soon as he started dabbing the herb over her wounds. "I need to talk to ... Luana." Her voice was a thin shrill, but she pushed through. "Luana?"

"I'm here." I stepped forward so she could see me. "You should save your strength. Let Keeran heal you. We can talk later."

She shook her head. "There's no time for that. I have to tell you ..."

I knelt beside her bed and took her frail hand. "Tell me what?"

"Isalia ... she killed Charles."

"W-what?"

"She has gone mad," she repeated her earlier words. "She wants a she-wolf pack so she killed most of the male wolves. She's keeping a few to procreate and keep the pack alive, but other than that, she's killing everyone, even the females that spoke against her." A sob cut through Macy's throat. "She killed my mate. I fought back, but she almost ended up killing me too. In the confusion, I escaped."

A pit opened in my stomach. When I thought things couldn't get worse ... "How did you find me?"

"I found a witch from the Silverblood coven when I was fleeing," Macy told us. "She was coming to check on things and report to Thea and Drake. She wanted to take me to the Silverblood estate, but I threatened her. I'm not proud of it, but I threatened her until she cast a tracking spell so I could follow you." She gestured down her body. "Only my wounds have been getting worse."

I shook my head, desperately helpless. "You should have gone to Drake and Thea. They would have helped you, healed you. They could have sent someone to find me."

A hollow chuckle turned into a hacking cough. Blood appeared on her teeth again. "I guess I was out of my mind. All that mattered was finding you."

But why me. "What can I do for you?"

She squeezed my hand, surprisingly tight for someone who was dying. "Not just for me. For all of the wolves who perished at Isalia's hands. Go back and kick her ass. Send that devil she-wolf back to hell and save our pack."

Tears brimmed in my eyes. "I'm going to try, but I'll find someone else to be alpha." I didn't know why I had told her that.

Macy's gaze became fierce, as if she suddenly had gained some clarity and strength. "I might not have seen it before, but you, Luana, you're the alpha our pack needs. I'm sorry I was too late to see it, but now with Isalia in command, I know you're much better than she and Ulric ever were. Please, save our pack."

"I will, but only if you let Keeran heal you." I stood and stepped back, giving Keeran some space.

Macy let out another strangled chuckle. "Don't waste your magic on me. I'm welcoming death." She closed her eyes and wrapped her hands over her stomach. "I want to meet my mate again."

I pressed a hand over my mouth to stifle a sob. Keeran

tended her, without healing, just helping her cope with the pain until she died.

With each passing minute, her heartbeat slowed and slowed, until it beat one last time.

Another sob rose in my throat and I hugged my middle. I had barely known this she-wolf. Yes, she had been part of my pack, but she hadn't been a friend. Why did it hurt so much to see her go like that?

Keeran stepped back and placed a hand on my shoulder. "I'm sorry."

Letting my guard down, I turned to him. He pulled me to him and wound his arms around me, hugging me tight.

And I cried in his arms.

WHILE I SHOWERED, I WONDERED WHY I HAD BEEN SO UPSET about Macy's death. All deaths upset me, but Macy's had hit hard. The only conclusions I came to were: Isalia defeating me; the others pushing me away after I told them she had cheated; Keeran rejecting me; learning the truth about how I became the alpha; betrayal welling in my core; Macy dying; and my pack descending into chaos and darkness.

I scrubbed my skin hard, trying to get rid of the dirt that had covered my body when we had buried Macy a couple of hours ago. If only it was that easy to erase not only dirt, but scary thoughts and crippling fear.

I didn't bother getting dressed after the shower. I crawled in bed in my birthday suit. I didn't feel like sleeping, but my body was too tired, my muscles still aching from that crazy fae magic and my mind turning sluggish. Even if I didn't sleep, I needed some rest before doing something about all the craziness surrounding us.

A knock came from the door. Slowly, I opened my eyes and was surprised with the light streaming into the bedroom through the window. I had slept? For how long?

The knock sounded again. "Luana?"

I quickly pulled the covers over my body. "Come in."

Keeran opened the door. His brows curled as he saw me in bed. "Were you asleep?"

"What time is it?" I asked, confused. I could have sworn I wouldn't have fallen asleep last night.

"It's almost noon." Wow, I had slept for hours. He started pulling the door closed. "Sorry. You must be tired. Go back to sleep."

"No, it's okay. I'm getting up." My hand moved to the edge of the blanket, but I remembered I was naked underneath, and stopped. For some reason, I didn't want him to see my bare skin right now.

"Right." Keeran stepped back. "I'll make some breakfast for you. Come down when you're ready."

He closed the door behind him and I let out a long breath. Would things ever be normal between us again? I doubted it. He had not only rejected me, but he had also lied to me. I didn't think a friendship could survive that.

I shot up from bed and donned some black leather pants and shirt I found in the closet. As promised, Myra had stocked the kitchen and given us more clothes while we were gone last night.

Did the witches know what we had been up to?

Not that it mattered.

After slipping my boots on and gathering my things—not

that I had much—I went downstairs. Wyatt, Farrah, and Keeran were in the outdated kitchen, seated around a rectangular table occupying the middle of the room. There was a fourth place set beside them with coffee, juice, eggs, bacon, and pancakes.

"Morning," I mumbled as I took my place. Had Keeran cooked all that for me? No, he probably had cooked for the four of us earlier this morning. I didn't need, or want, any special treatment.

"How are you feeling?" Wyatt asked me.

"I'm ... okay." I cut a piece of the egg and shoved it in my mouth. It was hot.

I glanced to their places. No plates, no food. They either had eaten long ago, or they didn't want to eat.

Which meant, Keeran cooked all of this for me.

"You seemed pretty hurt last night, though," the young wolf said. "You should rest more."

"I can make you a special brew," Farrah said. "It's like a tea, but it has special ingredients to quiet the mind and help you relax."

For someone who seemed to be hiding a lot from us, Farrah looked like part of the group now. I frowned at her, wondering what her goals were. Why was she here? She had her secrets, but she had saved us last night.

"I agree," Keeran said. "You should eat and go back to bed."

Why were they treating me like this? They had been in the fight last night too. Didn't they need rest and sleep?

I couldn't relax or rest for a second longer, even if my body was still sore.

I couldn't ignore it anymore.

I had to act.

I bit down the last of my pancakes and put my fork down. "I'm leaving," I told them.

Keeran nodded. "I thought you would want to go back to your pack after what Macy told you. I think you're right. Finding my mother and figuring out what to do about my father can wait. We should head—"

I raised my hand. "No, I mean, *I'm* leaving. You should stay and continue your mission." Hurt flashed in his eyes.

"You can't take Isalia by yourself," he said. I flinched at his words. "I mean ..."

"I know what you mean, but I think each of us has important tasks now." Despite all the pent up emotion inside me, I didn't have it in me to argue anymore. I was going to be as diplomatic as I could. "I believe Soren is a foe we can't ignore. If he is as bad as the Bonecrown witches say he is, then he'll eventually become a threat to the other witches, and to Drake and Thea, and to the Dark Vale pack too. The sooner you find him and figure out what you're going to do about your prophecy, the better." I didn't want to be mean, but I couldn't help it. I knew he was confused and lost about the prophecy —he didn't want to kill his father—but that wasn't my problem anymore. "And somehow I'll deal with Isalia before she destroys my pack and targets others." I stood. "I'll be leaving now."

Keeran shot up. "Luana."

"Wait." Wyatt jumped up, almost knocking his chair back. "If you're going back, I'm going with you. It's my pack too, you know."

"You'll be safer if you stay here," I said.

The young wolf shook his head. "I can't stay hidden here while you challenge Isalia alone. I'm going with you."

Slowly, Farrah stood too. "I'm ... going to stay and help Keeran."

I could see as Wyatt's heart shriveled with the news. He was hoping she was going with us.

I glanced from her to Keeran. "This is good. We have a team of two each." Who was I kidding? We still were pretty outnumbered no matter what. "Good luck to you two."

I marched out of the kitchen.

"Luana," I heard Keeran calling me, but I didn't stop.

"Wyatt, it'll be faster if we wolf out, so don't carry anything," I said, walking out of the manor, knowing he would hear me.

"Yes," he answered like a soldier.

Without stopping, I started taking my clothes off.

"Luana, wait." Keeran walked beside me, easily matching my strides with his long legs. "Just hear me out before you go."

Clenching my jaw, I halted and faced him. "What is it?" Even I could hear the sharp edge in my words.

He ran a hand through his hair. "I just ... I don't like the way you're leaving. I feel like this is more than goodbye."

He should have thought about that before rejecting me and lying to me. I let out a long sigh. If he didn't care about me the way I cared about him, it was fine. I couldn't force someone to like me. But the lying part ... I wasn't sure I could overcome that.

"I'm not sure what it is, but right now, I need some distance from you."

This time, Keeran flinched. "Luana ..."

"Goodbye, Keeran." I wolfed out, ripping the rest of my clothes apart in the process, and dashed away.

Once I crossed tree line, I slowed down and waited for Wyatt. But as soon as I heard Wyatt in his wolf form closing in on me, I transferred all my frustration and disappointment and rage to my paws and hit the ground hard as I left Keeran behind.

THE URGE TO GO AFTER LUANA AND WYATT DIDN'T LEAVE ME for many hours. Several times, I walked to the edge of the clearing surrounding the manor, intent on going after them. Although what Luana said about us separating and fighting our own enemies sooner rather than later was true, I didn't like the idea of letting her go that easily, especially because I knew she was going back to the pack with a hot head, and with Isalia even more dark and wild than before ...

I turned to the forest again.

"Don't go," Farrah said. She stood in front of the manor, just watching me as I gave in to my dilemma. Only to back away from it the next second. "She made it pretty clear she didn't want you to go after her."

I turned to the young fae girl. "I know her better than she knows herself. If she goes back to her pack like that, she's going to get herself killed."

"Wyatt will be able to talk her out of it before they get there," she said.

I tilted my head. "What do you mean?"

She shrugged. "He'll talk to her and she'll calm down, and then they will actually come up with a plan. Hopefully, they will also find some allies."

The Dark Vale pack was somewhat near the Silverblood estate and DuMoir Castle. If Luana was smart —and I knew she was—she would talk to Drake and Thea and request their help before marching in and confronting Isalia.

"I guess you're right." I stomped past her and into the manor.

Farrah followed me inside. "What about you? What are you going to do?"

I stopped in the middle of the foyer and looked up at the crystal chandelier covered in dust and cobwebs. "I don't know."

"Pretend I'm Luana and talk to me."

I stilled. I could never pretend anyone else was Luana, because Luana was special. Unique. I faced the young fae. "What are you doing?"

"Trying to make you talk about the problem," she said simply. "Whenever I'm in a bad situation, or even a bad mood, I talk about it. Even if I'm alone, I talk out loud as if I am telling my problems to a friend. Usually, I can find a solution, or at least a better path like that." She gave me an encouraging smile. "Try it."

I frowned. "I don't even know where to start."

"With whatever comes to mind first." She sat down on the stairs. "Here, sit down with me. Talking is better when seated."

What the hell was this girl doing? Did the fae study psychology like some humans did? It was the only explanation I had. Otherwise, why was a girl I had just met trying to make me spill my guts?

But maybe that was the charm in this. She was a stranger. I didn't care what she thought about me. And if the weight pressing in on me lessened, it would be worth it.

I sighed. "I have so many questions. About this damn prophecy and my mother ..."

"What about your father?"

I grunted. "Don't even get me started. Is he evil, or he isn't?"

"I guess it might depend on the point of view." She opened her arms wide. "If you ask me, the Bonecrown witches are all evil, and yet here we are. Staying at their place, eating their food, accepting their help." I frowned. "They are helping you. Being good to you. Good and evil isn't black and white, unfortunately. If it was, life would be much easier."

I stared at this young fae girl. To me, she looked to be sixteen, maybe even fifteen, but she spoke with the experience of a person much older than I was. Did fae age slower than witches and warlocks? One more thing I didn't know.

"If only there was someone whose magic was all seeing and could answer some of my questions ..."

Farrah raised her index finger. "Like a seer?"

"Something like that, yeah. Why?"

She stood from the stairs. "There's a seer in my brother's camp."

Although that was interesting, there was a little problem. "We're not welcomed there."

"The seer likes me. Since I was a little girl, she has been close to me. I could lure her away from the camp so she could talk to us." She blinked her long silver lashes at me. "What do you say?"

I didn't like how easy this sounded, but at the same time, I couldn't deny its appeal. "Do you think she'll be able to tell me more about the prophecy and where my mother is hiding?"

"If there's anyone who can, it's she." She stared at me, serious. "Look, I know you're probably wary of me, but you and your friends saved my life. I'm indebted to you and I really would like to help." She paused. "Besides, I'm tired of being alone."

I knew what she meant. I had been alone for a couple of months before, hiding and running from witches, were-wolves, and vampires, and I wished never to live like that again.

And this girl had been running for a while now, alone in the world.

Something inside me broke. "All right. Let's do this!"

As Farrah led the way through the forest, I tried clearing my mind of everything. I just wanted to find my mother and that was it. No prophecies, no destinies, no killing. I didn't want to be a Warlock Lord and reign over all warlocks. If I could, I would find my mother, then build us a cottage in the middle of nowhere and disappear from everyone's lives.

My chest tugged at the thought of not seeing Thea, Aurora, and Drake anymore. They had been a good part of my life. Great even. They had given me so much and helped me. I would miss them when I disappeared.

And Luana.

I wondered, if I asked her, if she would disappear with

me. No, probably not. Luana's wolf genes demanded she act and save her pack—even if that meant she would die trying.

But maybe if I helped her reclaim her pack, she could then appoint some other wolf as alpha, as she had mentioned before, and run away with me.

I shook my head. Knowing her, Luana would hold on to her grudge against me. Right now, she hated me and never wanted to see me again. She would never forgive me.

"What are you thinking?" Farrah asked.

From my calculations, we were close to the camp where the fae were yesterday. "About this seer of yours. What if she turns us in to your brother?"

"She won't," she assured me. "She always thought Daleigh was pompous and self-righteous, and she was always had a soft heart toward me. Don't worry, she'll talk to us."

But that didn't mean she had the answer I sought. Who cast the prophecy? Where was my mother and the warlocks who had run with her? Could I somehow change this prophecy? Could I ignore it?

Suddenly, Farrah skidded to a stop.

"What is it?" I asked, my voice low.

She shivered as if the air was too cold. "Something is wrong."

Slowly, we walked forward, until we were hiding behind the same tree and bush as last evening. I brushed the curtain of leaves aside and spied out.

I gasped. "Holy ..."

"No!" Farrah ran into the clearing, but her steps slowed the closer she got to them.

I followed her, my eyes on the destroyed huts, the smoldering fire, and the blood. So much blood. "What happened here?"

"I ... I don't know." A sob cut her words and she desperately looked around. Despite the amount of blood smeared everywhere, there were no bodies. Or at least, we hadn't found any yet. "Someone must have attacked them after we left."

I channeled my power, in case whoever did this still lurked nearby. "Farrah, we should leave."

She turned to me, her eyes glinting with the trace of tears. "But the seer—"

"Is probably dead," I said, my tone harsher than I intended. Farrah's lips turned upside down, and she put a hand over her stomach. "I have a feeling that if we don't go *now*, we're next."

"Too late," a voice said.

A magic bolt appeared in my outstretched palm as I turned in its direction.

Four men stood side by side, watching me with their dark eyes.

Farrah scurried to my side, and I felt as she called on to her magic too. "Who are they?" she asked in a low voice.

"I don't know." But I thought I knew *what* they were. Wearing black clothes that resembled a leather suit and a back cloak lined with dark red, I could bet these men were warlocks. "You did this?"

"Unfortunately," one of them said.

Farrah took a step forward, ready to attack. "You killed all of them?" I held her arm, not sure we should fight them. Not yet.

"Not all of them," the warlock said. "The majority managed to escape."

"But ... why?" Farrah shouted.

An amused grin spread over the warlock's features. "They wouldn't tell us where to find Keeran."

My stomach dropped. "You're looking for me?" Could ... could they be the warlocks who were hiding with my mother? But why would they kill the fae? "How do you know me?"

"You're Acalla's son," the warlock said. "We've been looking for you."

So it was true. "You know my mother? Where is she?"

The warlock shook his head. "No, no. I'm Virion and I work for your father, Soren. The Warlock Lord has extended an invitation for you to come to his manor."

My muscles tensed. "My father ..."

"The Warlock Lord has been watching you, Keeran," Virion said. "He invites his son to enjoy a feast with him tonight."

Farrah grabbed my arm. "This is a trap. Once you're in his clutches, he'll kill you. Just like these men killed my people."

"The fae have been threatening the warlocks for decades, just as the Bonecrown witches have," Virion said. "We were merely defending ourselves, like anyone would do in such a situation."

"Defending—" Farrah advanced toward them and I held her back again.

"Contrary to everyone's beliefs, the Warlock Lord isn't evil," Virion said. "He's just misunderstood." He fixed his eyes on me. "Keeran, are you coming with us?"

Was I going to the manor of a warlock who had been hunting me all my life just to kill me the moment his eyes landed on me? No, thank you.

Although, I confess, I hesitated. Like Farrah had mentioned, things weren't always black and white. Nobody was purely evil or purely good. There were too many shades of gray. It all depended from which angle you looked.

The way these warlocks talked about my father made me hesitate. What if he really wasn't evil? What if what the Bonecrown witches told me wasn't the whole truth? They could be wrong or mistaken or lying. What if my father had been searching for me and my mother to welcome us back? What if he didn't believe or care about the prophecy and just wanted his family back?

Hope bloomed in my chest, and yet, I couldn't force myself to say yes. "No," I finally uttered. "I'm not going."

I braced myself, ready for them to advance and take me by force.

Instead, they stepped back.

"It's all right," Virion said. "It was an invitation. The Warlock Lord would love to have his son with him for the feast, but he knew it wouldn't be easy to convince you."

"I wonder why," Farrah muttered.

"Don't worry," Virion said. "The Warlock Lord won't give up on his only son. Another invitation will come, and I sincerely hope you accept it then."

With that, Virion opened up his arm. Dark smoke rose from the ground, surrounding them.

A few seconds later, the smoke faded toward the sky.

The warlocks were gone.

IT WAS A LONG WAY BACK TO THE DARK VALE PACK, SO ONCE Wyatt and I went down the mountain, through the forest, and found a road, we followed it until we hit a small town, where we borrowed a car.

Neither of us said much of anything. I sensed Wyatt had started to develop feelings for Farrah and didn't like leaving her behind, but as a wolf of the pack, he couldn't just stay put. He had this maddening need to do something.

I knew because I had it too.

We drove for a couple of hours, but soon I heard Wyatt's stomach. It growled loudly—for my wolf ears—and then my stomach decided to reply.

He glanced at me. "I guess we're hungry." As part of wolf metabolism, we were always hungry. "Maybe we should do a quick stop for a bite."

I didn't want to waste time stopping and eating, but there was no way I could endure driving for hours and not eating anything. We could stop for a late lunch, then grab more food so we could eat in the car later.

"Okay," I muttered. "One quick stop."

At the next town, I veered off the interstate and followed the road until we found the first food joint: a small, family diner.

We left the car in the parking lot, praying nobody had reported it missing yet, and entered the diner.

"Welcome to MJ's Diner," a waitress said as she walked by us, carrying a tray full of drinks. "Sit anywhere you like. We'll be with you shortly."

I took a good sniff of the air before we moved any farther. Not that some supernatural couldn't disguise their scents, but right now, all I got were humans. The diner was full of humans.

Wyatt and I found a booth in a corner, from where we could watch almost the entire place. Despite the stolen car, I felt like we were fugitives on the run, and I want to keep an eye on anyone who could come for us.

The waitress, Carol, came and took our order: two burgers, a large portion of fries, and a milkshake for each of us. I also ordered some cold turkey sandwiches and plenty of cookies so we could take them for our snack later.

Wyatt and I remained in silence for the most part, only observing the clueless humans in the diner.

It was only after Carol handed us our food and I was done with the first burger when conversation started.

"Isn't it amazing how they really don't know about the supernatural world?" Wyatt asked, glancing around. "Don't you sometimes wish you were one of them?"

I frowned. "Are you saying you don't like being a wolf?"

"I'm saying it's not easy." He sipped from his milkshake. "I mean ... our world is bloody and dark and treacherous. You always have to watch your back, and all of a sudden friends turn into foes." His eyes fixed on a young couple two tables from our booth. "I wonder how it would be to live life when my biggest worry would be my grades in school."

I put down my half-eaten second burger. I couldn't say I hadn't thought about it and wondered how it would be to leave it all behind and live like a normal human, but at the same time, I couldn't imagine another life. "I bet they would love to have a taste of the supernatural. Have you seen how many books and movies they make about werewolves and vampires and witches? They would love to be us."

"Perhaps ..." Wyatt took a big bite from his burger and looked out the window. After he swallowed, he asked in a low voice, "We're doing the right thing, right?"

"What do you mean?"

"Separating from Keeran and Farrah." He returned his gaze to me. "I mean, I know taking Isalia out and finding Keeran's mother, not to mention figuring out what to do with his father, are important missions, but I still feel like we would be stronger together."

A pang of annoyance ran through me. "Then why did you come with me?"

"You might not be a true alpha, but you're still *my* alpha. I'll follow you no matter where you go."

Damn it, kid. This wolf had a way of twisting my gut in a way no one else could. "I appreciate your loyalty, but sometimes you have to think about yourself and do the smart thing." Even I knew this mission of mine was suicidal. I wouldn't win against Isalia, but if I could take her out, then another, better wolf could step up and become alpha. "You shouldn't have come with me."

"What else would I do? Follow Keeran into a warlock coven? I've had enough of witches and warlocks for a while."

I knew I had had enough of one certain warlock. I knew my temper was short because of him, because I let him affect me so much. And damn, I knew I shouldn't.

Before losing to Isalia, hadn't I been inclined to take a mate and produce pups to ensure the line of command in the pack? What would the rest of the pack think if I tried to force a mating bond with a warlock?

Shit, I was delusional.

Why was I even considering this?

Suddenly, something in the air changed. A dark feeling pressed against my back, and goose bumps raised the hair on my neck.

"Do you feel that?" I asked, looking around carefully.

Wyatt stiffened. "I do."

A moment later, the doors of the diner opened with a bang and their scent filled the place in no time.

Isalia and a dozen she-wolves strolled into the dinner like they owned the place. Isalia's eyes locked on mine instantly. Slowly, Wyatt and I got up.

"How can we help you?" Carol asked, a frown between her brows.

"Get lost." Bleiz, Isalia's right hand, pushed the girl aside, sending her flying across the entrance as if she was shooing a fly.

Immediately, other waitresses came forward, asking Bleiz and Isalia what the hell they were doing and telling them to leave. The customers in the diner got agitated.

"I'm calling the police!" someone shouted.

But Isalia wasn't paying attention to them. When her gaze

found me, a wicked smile spread over her mouth, revealing her elongated teeth. Several customers gasped.

"Luana, I've been looking for you," she said.

Isalia's wolves spread through the place, pushing the humans out of the way. They were surrounding us—Wyatt and me.

Damn it. All these innocent people would be caught in a bloody battle. I couldn't watch them die. "Go. All of you. Get out!"

The humans scrambled to their feet and made it for the door.

Isalia tsked. "Not so fast."

In the blink of an eye, Isalia's she-wolves shifted. The humans screamed in surprise and fear as they ran from the wolves. But they weren't fast enough. Isalia didn't move a muscle, only stared at me, while her wolves slaughtered the humans.

My stomach turned with such violence and so much blood. "Stop this!"

"But it's so much fun," she said, her wicked grin in place.

"What is it that you want? What are you doing here?" I asked, trying to get my bearings. The main door was behind Isalia, but there was the kitchen to my left. There was bound to be another door out that way. But I would have to break free through two wolves.

Other than that, there were the windows. If I threw a chair at one, the glass was sure to break, and Wyatt and I could run.

"I see what you're doing," Isalia said. "Trying to find an exit. Don't waste your time. There are more wolves outside. The moment you step out, they will kill you."

I clenched my fists. "Why were you looking for me? I

already lost to you. The pack is yours." Or whatever was left of it.

"Did you know you had some supporters among the pack? Oh yeah, some of them had the nerve of getting together and rebelling against me." She looked down at her nails, also elongated, halfway through a shift. "Of course, I killed them all. But then I realized there were probably more wolves who supported you; they were just being careful, bidding their time."

I shook my head at her. "You're mistaken. No one liked me in that pack." Well, with the exception of Wyatt, but he was right here beside me. Shit, I had to keep him safe from this crazy wolf.

"Oh, you would be surprised." She lowered her hand. "So, I decided to find the root of the problem and eliminate it." She didn't need to say anything else.

Instead, she shifted and advanced on me.

I only had time to get out of her way and yell, "Wyatt, run!" before she had rebounded and came at me again.

Two against thirteen—or more if she wasn't bluffing about the wolves outside. This was far from being a fair fight.

I shifted and jumped out of her way, just to run into two other wolves. Holy shit ...

The wolves advanced on me. I jumped, dodged, clawed, barrel through, bit down—after a couple of minutes, red stained the floor and chairs and tablecloth and I was sure the majority of the blood was mine.

A yelp echoed off the walls and my breath caught.

Wyatt.

I glanced up from my brawl, in time to see him being thrown to the side and hit the wall with a loud thump. He yelped again as his body fell to the ground.

Damn it! Instead of running, he had shifted and joined the fight.

Wyatt? Wyatt, answer me!

A groan echoed in my mind. That was enough for now.

Finding an opening, I took down the wolf in front of me, and jumped on a table. It flipped with my weight, giving me momentary cover.

I analyzed the situation. Somehow, Wyatt and I had taken down four wolves, which meant there were still nine who were eager to destroy us. And Wyatt was hurt.

Shit.

Isalia jumped over the table, and the she-wolves formed a half moon behind her.

This was it. This was where Wyatt and I were killed and my pack would be destroyed by a mad wolf.

To my surprise, Isalia let out a long groan. The other wolves lowered their heads and retreated a few steps.

What was going on? Isalia was giving me another chance? A challenge? Here? Like this?

Why?

I didn't have time to wonder more as she let out a short howl and lunged at me.

I skidded out of the way, and ended up bumping my side against a table's metal stand. The air was knocked out of me, and I saw stars for a moment. Isalia didn't waste time. She came at me again.

Forcing myself to focus, I got out of her way. But two feet later, I turned toward her. I had always been one to wait for the other wolf to come for me, so I would know which way to move first, but not this time. This time, I snarled and went for her.

Isalia was turning around when I charged her. Half

surprised, she didn't have time to move as I jumped her. She slid several feet back, until she was against a booth. She jerked, trying to get rid of me, but I didn't give her a chance. I bit down on her shoulder. A painful howl echoed through the diner.

This was it. This was when I killed this bitch and sent her to hell.

I went for her throat.

Isalia rolled around and kicked my stomach. Breathing hard, I wobbled back. Damn it! She had hit right beside the previous injury, and now my entire midsection was in screaming pain.

I shook my head and went back for her. I had to kill this bitch now.

That quick distraction had been enough time for her to flee.

But she didn't flee far. Instead, she turned and rushed at me.

Isalia rammed my tender side, pining me to a fallen table. I growled and tried turning my head to bite her anywhere, as long as she let go. But her paw came down on me, her claws sinking into my cheek and neck.

A yelp ripped through my throat.

Then that damned blade appeared between Isalia's teeth. Panic got a hold of me as this time I could clearly see a dark liquid dripping from it. Poison. The blade was laced in poison again. But for some reason, I didn't think this was a numbing poison.

This time it was a lethal poison.

Get ready, Wyatt spoke in my mind.

For what? The blade? The poison?

Isalia's eyes widened, and the blade disappeared from her

mouth when a spray of water hit her hind legs. She turned around and growled to Wyatt, who wobbled on all fours under the kitchen's door.

Fire billowed behind him. All of a sudden, the scent of burning food and smoke reached my nose along with the heat pressing on my mangled body. Because I had been so focused on the fight, I hadn't even noticed Wyatt had set fire to the kitchen.

Move because I'm gonna throw more oil on Isalia, he said.

Isalia bared her teeth at him.

Praying she wouldn't attack him before he was successful, I limped under a table and some chairs, grateful the smoke was spreading quickly and the she-wolves hadn't seen me.

I stopped and glanced back, just as Wyatt grabbed a pot handle with his jaw, then threw it on Isalia. Half of the oil spilled on the floor, but the other half hit her squared on the face and front legs.

She let out an angry growl and jumped on him.

Wyatt dodged Isalia's attack. When she turned around to get him again, she slipped on the oil and landed on her side.

Run! Wyatt shouted in my mind. *This place is gonna blow any second now.*

What?

Wyatt took off toward me. He paused long enough to slip his nose under my stomach and push me up.

I don't want to slow you down, I said. *Go ahead.*

As if.

He stayed by my side, pulling me up whenever my steps faltered. The smoke was now a thick cloud inside the diner and the heat from the fire was too much. We could hear the wolves howling, probably looking for Isalia.

I hated how I wished she got caught in the fire and died. All of them died.

Eons later, Wyatt and I escaped the diner. A crowd of humans surrounded it and a firetruck approached, its sirens ringing loudly.

A human man gasped and pointed at us. "Wolves! I told you there were wolves inside."

The crowd retreated, afraid of us.

Fine by me.

Let's go, I told Wyatt.

Pushing through the pain, I ran away from the crowd and the main street. Wyatt followed me, always a step behind, and I was sure he was being considerate. In case I fell, he would be right there to catch me.

We stopped in a narrow alley between two small buildings. I shifted back into my human form and leaned against a wall. Wyatt shifted a second later and knelt in front of me. His eyes glanced over my wounds.

"Damn, she got you good," he muttered.

"You think?" I tried snorting in a teasing way, but even that set a ripple of pain through my body and I couldn't do more than wheeze.

"I think when your healing kicks in, you'll be fine." He looked around. "I'm gonna find us some clothes." Closing my eyes, I nodded to him. I needed to rest for a little. Then, my healing would start and I would be all right. "Come on, Luana. Wake up. You can sleep later."

I spied Wyatt from under my lashes. He was already dressed in jeans and a T-shirt, and he had a bundle of clothes in his hands for me.

"That was fast," I mumbled.

"That took almost ten minutes." There was an edge to his

tone. He hastily pushed a shirt over my head and my arms through the sleeves. "Help me here. Fast before we're caught."

I didn't know why he bothered with clothes. I was covered in blood and would only stain whatever I put on.

But I knew he was right. We had to go. Because of that, I forced myself awake. It took a while, but I finished getting dressed in the ridiculous clothes Wyatt had gotten me, and after making sure no one was paying attention, we left the alley.

"We need a car," I said, looking down the street. Our previously borrowed car was currently parked at the diner, which was swarming with firefighters, policemen, and curious humans.

Wyatt jerked his chin to the side. "I think I see one."

There was a pickup truck in a house's driveway—and it was on, as if the owner was leaving, but then remembered something and went back inside to get it.

I hated stealing cars. It didn't make sense for a wolf to own one ... until you needed to travel long distances. Or you were hurt from a fight and needed to escape.

In no time, Wyatt slipped into the car and backed it from the driveway. I hopped on when he hit the street.

Just then, the owner marched out from the house. "My car! Stop!"

Wyatt sped away and we left the little town behind.

I lifted my bloody shirt and was glad to see the wound there was half healed already. But the other one ... I pressed my lips into a thin line and braced myself as I flipped the visor and looked on the mirror.

A nasty gash cut down my face, down my jaw, and halfway through my neck. Blood caked the wound, which meant healing had already started too, but it was going slow. This shit would leave a scar, I was sure of it.

Damn it.

Wyatt glanced at me from the driver's seat. "It doesn't look too bad."

"Right." I closed the mirror, disgusted by my appearance. Which was ridiculous. I had never been a vain woman before, and I wouldn't start now. I let out a long sigh, turning my mind to more important matters.

"What now?" Wyatt asked, as if reading my mind.

Good question.

Isalia had come with half the pack to attack me. I still didn't know why and how she had found us. What did that mean, though? That the rest of the pack was left alone back home? That the she-wolves Isalia brought with her were the only ones left in our pack?

More importantly, had she survived the fire in the diner?

I didn't know where this feeling came from, but I was sure Isalia hadn't perished. Evil didn't die so easily, so fast.

And she would come after me, right? Just like she did at the diner. Wherever I went, she would come after me, and I had to be prepared to meet her again.

Should we go back to our pack and see what was left? Try to gather forces to help us? Or should I go far and drive her away from our pack, to keep them safe from her clutches.

"I don't know," I told him.

And as if I didn't have enough problems of my own, my mind turned to another matter, another person who was probably struggling with his own three hundred problems.

What was Keeran up to? It had been only half a day, but so much could have happened. Had he found his mother? Or his father? Or learned more about the prophecy?

"You know," Wyatt started. "Maybe we should step back and rethink this. Regroup and strategize."

"You mean, find Keeran and Farrah again?" Why didn't that surprised me? Because he liked Farrah more than he admitted?

He gave me a sheepish grin. "Yeah. Perhaps splitting up wasn't a great idea after all."

If we had stayed together, Isalia would have found four of us, not two. With Keeran's and Farrah's magic, we were probably that much stronger. And Keeran, too, would be much stronger against whatever trouble he might find, if we stuck together.

My gut twisted. But did I want to see him again so soon after his rejection and lies? If I treated him as a business partner and nothing else, then perhaps I could endure it.

I sucked in a sharp breath. "All right. Let's find Keeran and Farrah."

18

MY NIGHT WAS RIDDLED WITH NIGHTMARES. IN MY DREAMS, I saw glimpses of my mother first running from my father, then hunting him. My father showed up too. At first, he was the evil guy, murdering every witch who crossed his path. Then, he changed and his home became some sort of sanctuary for weaker witches and warlocks who were running from evil beings.

In my dreams, I also saw Farrah fighting her people, Wyatt chasing me, and Luana so hurt, I didn't think she would make it.

When I finally pushed up from bed a little past six in the morning, I felt like shit. I took a quick shower, changed, and went downstairs to make breakfast.

I had no idea what to do next, but living in this house as if nothing was happening wasn't an option, and when Farrah woke up an hour later and met me in the kitchen, I told her that.

"Just tell me what to do and I'll go with you." She plopped down on a chair around the table, her eyes red and puffy.

After the warlocks left us last night, Farrah and I looked for survivors near her previous camp. There were none. They either all fled, or their bodies had been taken. We searched for them for a bit, but it was impossible. If I were them, I would have fled far from that site. She quietly cried the entire way back to the manor and didn't say a word as she retreated into one of the guest bedrooms.

I guess she had cried all night.

I handed her a steaming cup of coffee and sat across the table. "Are you okay? Want to talk about it?"

Sniffing, she wrapped her hands around the mug. "I don't even know why I care so much. They kicked me out, you know. I should hate them all."

I knew exactly what she meant. "They were still your family and your home before that. It isn't easy to forget and move on."

"Whatever." She sipped from the coffee. "I just need something to occupy my mind."

"I—" The clicking sound of the front door opening shut me up. Frowning, I rose to my feet. Was it Myra? She had come to check on us? "Who's there?" I started moving toward the foyer, but then two figures walked into the kitchen.

"It's us," Luana said.

I blinked, surprised to see them here. My surprise gave away to worry as I noticed the blood on their clothes.

Farrah shot up, looking at Wyatt. "What happened?"

"We were attacked by Isalia," Luana said. She had her long hair loose, and covering half of her face.

"What? Where? How?" I shook my head. "Are you hurt? Do you need healing?"

"No, we're fin—"

"Yes," Wyatt cut her off. "Luana needs healing on her face." He pointed to her weird hairstyle. "If you don't heal it, it'll leave an ugly mark."

Luana flinched.

I reached for her hair. "Let me see."

She slapped my hand away. "It's fine. It's ugly, but it's mine."

I stood my ground. "It might get infected or not healing properly. It happened before, remember? Let me see." This time, when I reached for her hair, she didn't stopped me, but she looked down, as if ashamed.

I did my best to hide my surprise, but I was sure she had heard my deep inhale. The thick, red gash cut through the middle of her cheek, down her jaw, to the middle of her neck. Blood caked most of it, but from what I could tell, her healing wasn't doing a good job and it would soon get infected, and once it did, the mark wouldn't go away.

"That bad, hm?"

I grabbed her shoulders and pushed her down into a chair. "I can heal it."

She snorted. "Don't lie to me."

Wyatt and Farrah slipped out of the kitchen while I grabbed my herbs from the counter.

"Well, I'll at least try my best." I pulled a chair closer and sat right in front of her. "This might sting a little," I warned her before applying the herb to the gash.

She hissed, but held on. I cupped her face, my palm pressing tightly against her wound, and sent a little of my magic into her, just enough to accelerate the healing process.

She lifted her hazel eyes to mine. My breath caught as I realized how close we were.

"I had never thought I was pretty before," she said in a low voice. "But now I'm sure I look hideous."

I pulled my hand back, but didn't move anything else. I glanced at the gash as it closed. It would heal and be better, but as it closed, a thin white scar stayed in its place. I returned my eyes to hers. How could she be so blind? "Luana, you could never be anything less than beautiful."

Clearing her throat, Luana pushed her chair back and stood. "It's done, right?"

"Yes." I frowned, remembering she was probably still mad at me. But if she was, then ... "What happened? What are you doing here? Why did you come back?"

She crossed her arms. It seemed she would remain in defensive mode around me. "Wyatt and I fought Isalia and her she-wolves at a diner. Wyatt set the place on fire, and we ran. Isalia and her wolves were inside, but I bet they didn't die. At least Isalia didn't, I'm sure." She paused. "And after Isalia's attack, Wyatt and I realized we are stronger together. The four of us."

I nodded. "To be honest, I think so too." Especially now, seeing as Isalia had come after Luana like that. If that she-wolf hadn't died in the fire, she would certainly come after Luana again.

"This is merely a partnership," Luana said quickly. "Once you find your mother and do whatever you need to do with your father, and I take Isalia down, we can each resume our own obligations."

She meant we could each turn around and walk away from each other. What else could I expect after all I had done to her?

"Sounds good," I said, my voice low.

"So ..." She walked past me and grabbed an empty mug from the cupboard. "What is our next step?"

I straightened in my chair and leaned my elbows on the table. "I don't know." I told her about what had happened last night—going after the fae seer, seeing Farrah's camp destroyed, the confrontation with the warlocks ... "Part of me thinks we should stop running and go to Soren before he comes after me."

Luana's brows curled down. "That doesn't sound like a bad idea. We're acting first, instead of remaining here like sitting ducks. I like it." She filled the mug with coffee. "Who knows? Maybe what Queen Corvina told us about him is wrong, or twisted. Maybe he's a kind man who wants to find his love and his son."

How I wished those words were true, but something in my gut told me they weren't. "Are you sure you want to come with me?"

Luana stilled for a brief second. Then, she set her untouched coffee down. "I'm sure. Let's get ready. The sooner we go, the sooner all of this is done."

She marched out of the kitchen.

A painful pang cut through my chest. What she meant was, the sooner we were done, the sooner she would be able to walk away from all of this.

From me.

19

LUANA

ALTHOUGH WYATT AND I HAD TAKEN A NAP INSIDE THE TRUCK in the middle of the night, before abandoning it and hiking through the forest, we were still tired. Since there was no real rush for anything, though I wanted to finish all of this as soon as possible, Keeran suggested Wyatt and I sleep for a couple of hours before proceeding.

I didn't argue. I slept for almost three hours, then took a shower, checked my wounds—it was hard to admit, but the thin white scar on my face bugged the hell out of me—and changed into clean clothes and boots. Being a werewolf was great, but the amount of clothes I had already lost in the past few days was troublesome. If only Keeran could cast a spell that allowed me to always carry a bag with extra clothes even in wolf form, or a spell that made clothes appear on my body each time I shifted back to human.

I shook my head. Why was I thinking about spells and Keeran?

When I went downstairs, I found a plate with sandwiches in the kitchen.

"Our lunch," Farrah said, taking one. "After we eat, we're leaving."

I took a sandwich. "Where's Wyatt and Keeran?"

"Keeran is outside, already waiting, and Wyatt is getting dressed." Her cheeks gained a rose tint. She had either been with him while he changed, or she had walked in on him. Either way, she had probably seen Wyatt and his muscles. He was a handsome young wolf; I couldn't blame her for thinking he was attractive.

I finished eating my sandwich, grabbed two more, and walked out of the house, my mouth full.

Keeran sat on the porch steps, his eyes on the bright blue sky. He was so lost in his own thoughts that he hadn't seen me as I walked closer. He also didn't see as I stared at him, at his golden skin, his chocolate-brown hair, at the sharp angles of his chin and nose. Even mad at him, I could admit he was handsome, more than any man should be allowed.

He wore pants and shirt and vest that reminded me of a combat uniform, and paired with his cloak, it made him look like one hot, badass warlock.

My heart squeezed. Why did he have to lie to me? To betray me like that?

The door opened behind me, and Wyatt and Farrah walked out.

Keeran woke up from his stupor and glanced at us. "Ready?"

Had we ever been ready for any of our missions? I doubted it. And yet, we never let that stop us.

Without a word, I walked past him.

Farrah and Wyatt exchanged a look, then followed me. "We're ready," Wyatt said.

Sighing, Keeran grabbed a bag from the ground and slung it over his shoulder. "Then let's go."

———

As Queen Corvina had told us, the Dark Witch Manor wasn't far from the Bonecrown coven, and we entered warlock territory in a matter of hours.

Warlocks—men wearing dark leather suits and long cloaks lined in burgundy—stepped from the shadows moments after we crossed the border.

"Glad you came, Keeran," one of them said.

Beside me, Keeran nodded. "Yes, Virion, I'm a day late, but I came." So, this was Virion, one of the warlocks who had paid Keeran and Farrah a visit last night. Something about him didn't sit well with me. I couldn't tell if it was his eyes or the easy smile on his lips, but I instantly didn't like him. "I've brought my friends with me." Keeran gestured to us. "Luana, Wyatt, and Farrah."

Virion's nose wrinkled. "We don't usually allow supernaturals, but if they are your friends, then they are ours too." He beckoned us forward. "Come. I'll take you to the manor."

We followed Virion down a narrow stone path that weaved among the trees before opening to a wide hill. A dark gray stone mansion and its tall towers stood proud atop the hill.

"The Dark Witch Manor," Keeran whispered.

I shuddered.

What was that eerie feeling?

"This way." Virion took us up the path and into the manor.

Wherever we looked, warlocks filled the rooms. They played instruments in a music room, read books in the library, and gathered around a table to debate subjects. A group walked by us, talking about going to the gym to exercise. Another group spoke of cooking lessons tomorrow morning. They looked like disciplined scholars.

And when we crossed their paths, they all stopped whatever they were doing and turned to us. All of them were dressed in dark clothes, mostly black, and some wore cloaks —short or long, but always black. But the most curious part was that every one of them bowed their heads when we walked past.

They bowed their heads to Keeran.

Was he regarded as some kind of prince?

I was about to tease Keeran about it, but when I looked at him, the words died on my tongue. With wide eyes and his lips curled upward, Keeran took in everything. He seemed as excited as a kid at an amusement park.

My stomach sank.

Keeran was enjoying this. He was delighted to be among so many warlocks.

Suddenly, I wondered if coming here had been a mistake.

———

VIRION SHOWED US TO FOUR SUITES ON THE THIRD FLOOR.

"Please, rest here," he said. "Keeran, I'll let your father know you're here. I'll come for you when supper is ready."

Just like that, he marched away, leaving us alone in the corridor.

I frowned as I watched him backing away. That was it? No warlock guards, no instructions, no "don't walk around on your own." Nothing?

The heavy, weird feeling in my gut only increased.

Farrah grabbed Wyatt's hand and disappeared inside a suite. Smiling, Keeran entered another one. Still wary, I followed him inside.

"Isn't this great?" He gestured to the room. What did he want me to see? I wasn't one for decoration. To me, if it had a bed, comfortable sheets, and a dresser to keep my things, I was fine. Keeran went to the long window and looked down. "Did you see? There are only warlocks here."

Which was strange. Queen Corvina had told us Soren's warlock coven had a few females, who were kept for procreation. Since we hadn't seen any, I wondered if they were treated like cattle and locked away.

Like slaves.

I shuddered again.

"I'm not sure great is the right word for it," I said. If I wasn't careful, I would end up hurting him, aggravating him.

He turned to me, his smile fading. "What do you mean?"

I shrugged. How did I say this? "It looks ... too perfect. Like they knew you were coming and prepared a show for it." Hence the warlocks walking freely around and the beautiful suites. Soon, gorgeous women would bring him food and even bathe him. Ugh. "I don't like it."

"I'm not sure I agree with you." He looked past the window, to the setting sun and the orange staining the sky on the horizon. "This place feels different than I expected. Perhaps Queen Corvina was mistaken. Perhaps she doesn't know the entire truth."

Perhaps you're letting your guard down and being enchanted by things that are meant to trap you.

"Keeran ..."

He looked at me again, his eyes shining bright. "I want to give my father a chance, Luana."

I froze, realizing I had lost him.

Shit, for his sake, I really hoped he was right.

My brain went numb after that, and as much as I tried to come up with words that would make sense, that would make him see what I saw, nothing came to me. I tried putting myself in his shoes. My parents died when I was a pup, but if I found out they were alive, and one of them might be evil, I guess I would want to give him the benefit of the doubt too, no matter what. After all, he was still my parent.

A knock came from the open door.

Keeran and I spun around.

"Ready, Keeran?" Virion asked. "Your father is waiting for you."

As I followed Virion down the stairs, I did my best to push Luana and her strange behavior out of my mind. I guess that, as a (former) friend and a wolf with a short temper, she was naturally wary of everything and everyone. Being in a castle with hundreds of warlocks? That had to set every nerve in her body on high alert.

I tried to understand, but right now, I was overwhelmed. Even though the sun was setting, it didn't seem the warlocks were slowing down and settling in for the night. There were still plenty of warlocks milling around the rooms, discussing history and math and magic, talking about human sports and news, playing instruments, reading.

This place was surreal.

Virion gestured to a large stone archway to the side. "Through here." I walked in with him, but after two steps, I skidded to a stop.

The room was impressive: shiny black wooden floors, light gray walls covered with paintings of dark mountains and forests, a long black stone table, and twelve chairs with light gray cushions.

But the most impressive thing was the man standing on the other side of the room.

The moment his eyes met mine, I knew. This was him. This was Soren, my father.

"Keeran," he said in an exhale.

He marched to me, and I him. He looked like me, or I looked like him. He had the same dark brown hair, but his was longer, past his shoulders, and his eyes were the same brown as mine. Like me, he was tall and built, but he had a thin beard covering his chin and jaw. And he emanated pure magic. I could feel it coming off him in waves.

He stopped right in front of me, his eyes fixed on mine.

"My lord," Virion said, bowing his head. "This is Keeran, your son."

I had doubts. Queen Corvina had warned me this man wanted to kill me. The moment he found me, I was dead. And I had brought myself to him, wrapped like a little gift.

Had I gone insane?

But when Soren reached for me and clasped my arm with both his hands in a tight squeeze, his lips breaking into a grin, I let all the worry disappear.

"My son." He tugged me closer and embraced me. "You're here. Finally, I've got you back." I remained frozen, lost. Still smiling, he pulled back. "You're taller than I imagined. Stronger too."

I didn't know what to say to him. Until recently, I hadn't considered the possibility that I had a father, that he was still alive. Besides the things I had heard from Queen Corvina, I had no ideas or hopes for him.

Until now.

His smile, his eyes, his excitement upon seeing me—it was all true. I could feel it.

Would he feel that way if all the wanted was to kill me?

I doubted it.

Before I could manage to say anything, more warlocks entered the room.

"So, this is your son, my lord?" a short warlock with cropped black hair asked as he approached us.

Soren turned to him. "Yes, Tack, this is Keeran, my beloved son."

"Keeran?" one of the warlocks asked. "I thought his name was Esmund."

Soren straightened. "That was the name I chose for him when he was born, yes. Esmund." He glanced at me. "But I can see your mother was right. Keeran does suit you better." Wait a minute. Keeran hadn't always been my name? It was supposed to be Esmund. Not noticing my shock, Soren gestured to the warlocks who formed a half circle around us. "My son, this is Bates, Tack, Damien and Eldon, my closest friends and trusted advisors."

"Welcome to the Dark Witch Manor, Keeran," Bates said. He was tall and lean with long blond hair. With his delicate features, he looked young. An advisor? Well, maybe warlocks aged differently. Although, I haven't felt anything yet.

"Thank you," I forced out, my voice a little shaky.

"Come on." Soren gestured to the table. "Let's sit down. Supper will be served soon."

Soren took the largest chair at one end of the long table. I was offered the chair to his right, while Virion took the one on his left. The other four warlocks divided themselves in two and took Virion's and my side.

Not a moment later, a side door opened and five people came in—three women and two men.

Humans.

I stared in shock as I saw healthy humans wearing elegant uniforms, serving us drinks and placing first-course plates in from of us as if they were hired workers, not slaves.

Could they really be free here?

I studied them as they leaned closer, pouring red wine in the goblet in front of me. No marks around their wrists and neck. No sign of any wounds or abuse. Curious, I glanced around. There were no guards or extra warlocks positioned along the walls or room entrances. I mean, I was sure the six warlocks seated at the table with me were more than capable of defending themselves should the necessity arise, but still, I didn't think I ever saw a lord or a queen without an entire security team behind them.

Unless the five warlocks seated at the table with us were that security team.

Easy, simple conversation rolled around the table as the humans stepped back and the warlocks waited for Soren to take the first bite. They talked about their spell classes and mentioned some students and their levels, and about a new class a certain instructor wanted to try out.

I felt like I had stepped into a boarding school for magic users, and I desperately wished I had found this place about ten or fifteen years ago.

After the second course was served, Soren lifted his hand. Conversation died instantly.

"I would like to know more about my son." He turned his dark eyes to me. "Tell me about your life, Keeran."

I cleared my throat, suddenly not liking the spotlight.

"There's nothing much to tell. I was raised at the Silverblood coven and—"

"Wait," Bates interrupted. "Doesn't the Silverblood kill the males born from witches?"

"That was before the new queen took over," Eldon said. "She welcomes them."

"But how did you survive, then?" Tack asked.

I told them what I thought was the truth: My mother had found a way of suppressing my magic and I lived at the Silverblood coven as a human. That sparked a little outrage from Soren, who asked me about being used as a sexual slave.

"I would rather not comment on that." I looked down at my plate, ashamed of my past. Before they could ask more about that, I told them how Thea became my friend and saved me from that life. "Thea is a great witch queen, and Aurora will be the best Queen of All Witches someday."

The warlocks exchanged glances.

"Do you know if Queen Thea has any plans for us?" Virion asked, his tone guarded.

"I don't know," I confessed. "Thea found out about the existence of a warlock coven when I did. It was a shock to her too. I'm sure she won't make any rash decisions, though. She'll certainly wait for a report from me before taking any action, be it an alliance or an attack."

Soren nodded. "This queen sounds wise indeed. I would love to meet her someday."

For some reason, that didn't sit well with me.

I straightened in my chair and went direct to the point. "Queen Corvina of the Bonecrown coven seemed to be under the impression I wouldn't be welcome here, that there is a prophecy." The other five warlocks went rigid and lowered their heads as if trying to disappear. "Tell me about that."

Soren shook his head. "I'm sure everything you heard about me thus far has been a lie."

"So there's no prophecy?"

"No, there's a prophecy, but the only thing the prophecy says is that someday you'll become the Warlock Lord, and you'll be the strongest warlock to ever walk this Earth." He shrugged. "Wouldn't that be expected? I mean, a crown prince takes over for a king after he dies. Unfortunately, warlocks don't live forever, and someday you will take over for me."

"But ... Queen Corvina said—"

He tsked. "Corvina is a crazy, evil little witch. We've had problems for centuries. They like blood rituals and keep picking off our workers, poor humans."

"She also wants to expand her territory," Virion added.

"Right." Soren nodded. "She has been pushing the border of her territory for over a century now, trying to steal some of our land. Of course, we fight back. I won't let her steal our land! We don't like the Bonecrown witches and they don't like us. It doesn't surprise me that Queen Corvina lied to you about all that."

I frowned. Now what? Who was telling the truth? "It's just ..."

Soren reached across the table and rested his hand on mine. "Keeran, all I wanted in life was to find the love of my live and our beloved son. Finally, I have found you, and hopefully the both of us can find your mother."

Speaking of which ... "If that is true, then why did my mother flee with me?"

"Another one of Corvina's lies." Soren grunted. "She didn't flee. She went on a trip with you. You were a few months old, and she wanted to introduce you to her coven. I told her not to go because most of the covens weren't accepting of warlocks, but she went anyway." He paused, his eyes shining with what looked like unshed tears. "And she never returned. I don't know what happened to her. Nobody does."

"W-what?"

"We believe your mother was kidnapped by some other supernatural group," Virion said. "That's the only conclusion we got after searching for so long and not finding one miserable clue about her."

"We heard she showed up at the Wildthorn and the Bonecrown covens," Soren said. "But when we went after her, she wasn't there." He placed a hand on his chest. "It kills me, living every day for the last twenty something years and not knowing what happened to your mother. What had happened to you."

I stared at him, his words bringing forth feelings I didn't know I had. A deep longing hit me hard, and I wanted to believe him. Because would there be anything more wonderful than having a family? The three of us together?

But I couldn't help also feeling skeptical. Since discovering I was a warlock, I had seen Thea and Drake betrayed by people they trusted, and I had seen plenty of supernaturals who lied, even little lies, for their advantage.

No one was perfect or purely good.

I knew that well.

But what was Soren? I couldn't tell. Not yet.

"To be honest," I started. Half a dozen pairs of eyes fell on me, and I felt their pressure. "I'm—"

"It's okay," Soren cut me off. "I know how you must feel. Confused and lost. I get it." He pulled his hand back. "Why don't we put this subject aside and finish dinner on a lighter note."

"Great idea, my lord," Eldon said.

He snapped his fingers and the humans advanced. They changed our plates, serving us the next course.

"Keeran, I won't touch on this subject anymore tonight, but I would like to tell you one more thing," Soren said. "My dream is to have my family back by my side and rule our coven together. Even if we search high and low and never find your mother, I would like you by my side. Think about it." A big smile spread across his lips and he looked down at his plate. "Now, this looks delicious. Let's eat."

Soren and the other warlocks dug in. I picked up my fork, but I had lost my appetite.

AT FIRST, I WAITED IN MY BEDROOM. I TOOK A LONG BATH, changed into nice clothes (the closet here had *everything* in it), was brought a nice dinner (which I sniffed first, searching for any kind of poison), paced around the room, and looked at the moon through the window ... But as the hours stretched, I went to Keeran's room and waited for him there.

I sat in front of the window and waited.

And waited.

And waited some more.

Finally, after hours, I heard his footsteps at the end of the corridor. I shot up, then sat back down and forced myself to relax in the chair, lest he think I was worried.

Which I wasn't.

Right ...

Keeran slipped into the room and halted, his brows furrowing upon seeing me there. "Hey."

Who was I kidding? He knew I was dying here. I shot to my feet as he closed the door. "So? How was it?"

He took a few steps toward me, but halted three feet away. "It was ... different than what I expected."

I crossed my arms. "Tell me."

And he did. He told me about how strong his father looked, about how the other warlocks seemed to respect and love him. He told me about the incredible food he ate during dinner, about the human workers—and he emphasized they were not slaves—and he told me about what his father said.

"My father said he was looking for me and my mother, so he could get his family back. He says he wants us by his side. He wants me to stay here and help him search for my mother."

"And you believe him?"

"I know it sounds crazy after what we heard about him from Queen Corvina, but he explained to me the Bonecrown coven has had problems with the Dark Witch Manor for decades. Queen Corvina would lie to get me on her side."

"And you believe him?" I asked again. Because he certainly wasn't in his right mind right now.

Keeran ran a hand through his messy hair. "Look, I know, okay? I know, but ..." He took another step toward me. "What if it's the truth? What if Queen Corvina is truly evil and likes to eat babies for snacks and drink their blood as wine—" My stomach turned in disgust. "—and she's been trying to get the Dark Witch Manor lands for centuries? We don't have any reason to believe her over my father."

"We didn't really believe her ..."

"So you believe my father?"

"That's not what I'm saying. What I mean is, there could be a third side to this story. Don't pick a side just yet."

He let out a long sigh. "But this is my father, Luana, and he talks about my mother as if he adores her."

What was I supposed to say to that? From where I was standing, Keeran had already made his choice. He was just having trouble admitting it. "So, you're staying." Which meant I was going back to my pack alone with Wyatt, as we originally planned. Why had I bothered to come back?

"That's not what I'm saying." He pressed the heels of his hands to his eyes, and his head drooped. "I'm just ... so lost. So confused."

Seeing a man his size admit he was lost and confused gutted me. Without thinking, I closed the distance between us and embraced him—even if I was still mad at him. Right now, he needed a friend, and despite everything, I could be that friend for him.

"It's okay," I whispered. "We'll figure this out together."

He rested his head on my shoulder and wound his arms around my waist, pulling my body tight against his. Every nerve of my body came to life, and when he inhaled deeply, his nose brushing against my skin, my heart thundered against my chest.

Holy shit ...

His nose trailed up my neck, and his lips brushed across my jaw, sending a delicious shiver down my spine. "Tell me and I'll stop," he whispered, his lips right at my ear.

Moon be damned, I should tell him to stop. I really should.

But I was so far gone.

I clutched my hands around his shoulders, locking him in place and turned my face to his. "Don't stop," I whispered back.

Keeran pulled back an inch, his eyes searching mine. What was he looking for? Then he closed his eyes, pressing them tight, and shook his head. "I ..."

My temper rose again, but before I could get mad, it hit me. Oh, I knew what was going on. He had confessed before that every time he closed his eyes, he saw the witches who had abused of him. And now, when he thought he was finally ready to forget them, they came back to haunt him.

I brought my hands up and cupped his face. "It's okay," I whispered. I stood on my tiptoes and planted a soft peck on his cheek. "It's just me." I pressed my lips to his other cheek. "You know me." I touched my lips to the tip of his nose. "I'm right here."

Slowly, he opened his eyes, those endless chocolate pools locked on mine. I saw the shift in him, when he chose to push those painful memories aside and allow new, happier ones.

A hint of a smile appeared on his lips. The next second, one of his hand cradled the nape of my neck and his mouth crushed mine. I gasped in surprise, but when I felt his warm lips moving against mine, I let it all go.

I melted into him, into his kiss, into his strong arms, into his whole being. I had been kissed before, but not like this. Not like a mouth had been made to fit mine, not with this perfectly frantic rhythm, not with this heat rising inside me, threatening to burn me alive.

Keeran pushed me back a few steps, until my back was pressed against the wall beside the window, my body happily trapped and glued to his. I savored his kiss, the tease of his tongue, the bite of his teeth, while I trailed my hands around his shoulders, down his chest, trying to explore his ripped muscles as much as could.

If only he had no clothes on.

I brought my hands lower and slipped them under this shirt, my nails scratching on the sides of his six-pack.

Keeran hissed against my mouth before deepening the

kiss, ripping a gasp from my lips. He grasped my hips and pressed his body against mine on all the right parts. I felt his erection against my lower belly and my throat went dry.

By the moon ...

Pure heat spread through my body, too fast to process. I succumbed to it, and in my delirious state, I clutched his shoulders again, this time bringing myself up, and aligning myself with him. I moved my hips against his erection.

Keeran let out a string of whispered curses before drawing his lips over my new scar. I stilled for a moment, suddenly self-conscious about the thing marring my skin. "So beautiful," he whispered. "This doesn't change anything. You're still too beautiful to be true."

My heart skipped a beat, then sped up, beating so fast that I thought it would burst out of my chest. And just like, I forgot about the scar. And when he dragged his mouth back to mine and kissed me again, and moved his hips in rhythm with mine, I was sure I was about to forget even my name.

A tug started deep in my chest. I mistook it as just another side of my lust and didn't pay any attention to it at first, but as I kissed Keeran and his hands ran down my body, the tug increased and took over my entire heart to the point where it was hard to breathe.

Moon be damned.

It was the bond. The mating bond. It had clicked into place.

With Keeran.

Shocked, I dropped my legs and pushed him back.

"What's wrong?" he asked, not resisting me, but not pulling back either.

Averting my eyes, I snaked out of his arms and took a few steps back. "I'm just ..."

What should I say to him? I couldn't tell him he was my mate. I was a werewolf. He was a warlock. We weren't supposed to be. But we were. The bond said so.

He tilted his head. "Luana, talk to me."

I shook my head, too confused to utter a single word. How could a werewolf mate with a warlock? If I had plans of being a lone wolf, maybe it wouldn't matter, but wasn't I planning on taking my pack back from Isalia? The other werewolves would never accept a warlock, especially as the alpha's mate.

This wasn't right.

The tug cut through my heart, strong and sure. Then why did it feel so right?

"I ..." I snapped my mouth shut. I had to think of some excuse and fast.

Keeran let out a long breath. "I get it." I stared at him. What? "You're still mad at me about what happened and for lying to you about your fight against Ulric. Believe me, I get it."

"R-right," I said. By the moon, this was such a terrible lie. I mean, yes, I was still mad at him for that, but I didn't think that would have stopped me from going further with him tonight. "I need some time."

"I understand." Keeran nodded.

I took a step back, aiming for the door. "I'm going to—"

"Just hear me out before you go." Holding my breath, I halted. He took a step closer, then back, as if remembering I needed space. "I already said this, but I need you to hear it again. I'm so sorry for lying to you and helping you win against Ulric. It was never my intention to break your trust and have you hate me. I only did what I thought I had to so as not to lose you. And ..." He walked to the nightstand beside the bed. He opened the drawer and drew the crystalized rose from inside. I sucked in a sharp breath. "I like you, Luana. For real. I hope you can forgive me. I also hope you'll be open to how I feel about you." He offered the rose to me.

I shouldn't take it. I shouldn't ... I took the rose from him and cradled it against my chest as if it was the most precious of my possessions. "Thank you," I whispered. "For the rose."

He nodded.

Before I did something stupid, like finish what we had started earlier, I whirled on my heels and dashed from the room.

I locked myself in my bedroom and leaned against the door, breathing hard. By the moon, what had happened? I glanced at the rose in my hand, and my heart tugged with pure longing, pure desire ... pure love.

As if I didn't have enough problems to deal with, I was now mated to a warlock. My pack would never accept that.

But what if I stayed here with him? A shudder rolled down my spine. No, that wasn't a possibility. Keeran might not see it, but these warlocks weren't the saints he believed they were. There was something fishy going on here, he just couldn't see it yet.

He didn't want to admit it, but I knew he had already made up his mind. He was staying with his father.

And I had to go on by myself.

Once more, fate was a twisted, sick little thing. I had finally felt the mating bond, but it was with someone I couldn't be with.

22

I DIDN'T SLEEP WELL. I BLAMED MY MIND AND THE MANY thoughts inside it. My mother, my father, the prophecy, Luana.

Luana.

Most of the night, I tossed and turned because of her. Because of the freaking great kiss we had shared, because I had felt her desire for me, just as much as I desired her.

Because she had pulled away and left me alone in this cold bed.

I didn't blame her. After all I had done to her, I didn't even think she would kiss me, not yesterday, not ever. She surrendered to lust for a few minutes, but she soon came to her senses and left.

As she should.

Luana was too good, too perfect for a hot mess like me.

Early morning, a human worker brought me breakfast, and I could only assume he had brought food for Luana, Wyatt, and Farrah too. I wanted to go check on her, but I was afraid she was still shunning me out. I didn't even go check on Wyatt and Farrah, afraid they would all be together.

And I was here alone.

Pitting myself.

I was so freaking stupid.

A freaking grown man who had finally broke through the emotional curse those evil witches had left on my soul, who had finally let go of the monsters of the past and made peace with himself, and here I was, hiding in my room like a coward.

That was it. I was going to talk to her. Even if she still needed space, I had to make sure she understood my feelings for her. I turned to the door, intent on marching across the hall and bang on Luana's bedroom, when a knock came from my door.

I blinked, then raced to open it.

It was Luana. She had thought about it and she had something to say.

My heart sped up as I reached for the knob. But once I opened and saw Virion standing on the other side, my shoulders sagged.

"Good morning, Keeran," Virion said, sounding way too chipper for early morning. "Your father is out for a stroll in the gardens, and he was wondering if you would like to join him."

I still hadn't decided what to do about my father—and everything—but I could use some time away from this bedroom, away from Luana, so I wouldn't go after her before she was ready to talk.

"Yes, I would like that." I closed the door behind me and followed Virion down the stairs.

On the way to the gardens, I once more saw many

warlocks in the adjacent rooms—studying, playing, talking, laughing ... I frowned. This was a place of learning, of friendship, of growth. It couldn't be as bad as Queen Corvina made it sound.

On the last set of stairs before the back porch, a group of teenagers carrying books walked by us. They stopped and bowed to me. I raised my hand in greeting, still feeling awkward with the entire bowing thing.

"Get used to it," Virion said. "They grew up hearing about Esmund, the long-lost son of the beloved Warlock Lord. Soren talked so much about you, you might as well be a saint to all of us."

Could someone get used to that? I didn't want to be revered as a saint. I just wanted to be one more among them.

The chilly air of the mountains greeted us when we stepped out on the back porch. The sun was already high, indicating it wasn't as early as I first had thought. It shone on the vast green lawn. In the distance, I could see a reflection pool straight ahead, a colorful flower garden to the right, and an orchard to the left. And beyond all that, tall trees from the forest flanking the mountain.

This place was too beautiful to be an evil lair.

Virion stopped at the end of the porch and gestured to the stone path leading to the orchard. I narrowed my eyes, but then I saw the flutter of dark robes beyond the tree line.

"Thank you," I said, before taking the path.

For a moment, I was curious why Virion would stay behind, but decided it didn't really matter. As I had observed last night, Soren never had any guards with him.

As I walked down the path, I noticed the trees—apple, peach, pear, and cherry—were set up in a square grid, giving the impression of forming endless green corridors.

I crossed a few apple trees and found my father, walking leisurely—his hands behind his back, his eyes exploring the tops of the trees or the blue sky.

"I like walking among the trees," he said, his back to me. "It helps me clear my mind, organize my thoughts. It relaxes me."

"I hadn't taken you for a nature lover."

Soren turned to me with a half-smile. "Nature is life, and life is magic." He wiggled his finger toward a green apple. It changed colors, becoming orange and then a bright, dark red. "Like this."

Seeing another male doing magic ... it was incredible. All my life, I had believed only witches existed and practiced magic. Then, I thought I was the only warlock in the world. And now, here I was, surrounded by dozens of men like me.

I wasn't alone anymore.

"This place is magical." The words flew out of my mouth before I could register them.

Soren nodded. "It sure is." He beckoned me to follow him. We weaved through some trees until we reached a small clearing with stone benches. Like a secret place amid the orchard. He sat down on a bench and patted the stone beside him. A little wary of where this was going, I sat down near him. "I can't help feeling eager and just ... content that you're here." He turned to me. "Now that you're here, so much can change. We can do so much. Together."

I liked the sound of the word together. "What do you want to do?"

"What do you know about our history?"

I shook my head. "Not much. All I know is that warlocks ruled over the witches, until the witches became too many and took over. A war ensued, and you and your warlocks were pushed back." I paused. "Queen Corvina mentioned all you want is to hunt down the witches and kill them all, so you and your coven can rule over all warlocks and witches again."

Soren clicked his tongue and looked down. "Of course she would say something like that." A long sigh escaped through his lips. "The truth is, witches and warlocks lived together in a harmonious society many centuries ago. The covens were mixed, like the human world is. Female and male together, no one counting heads to know who was winning." His brows slammed down. "Until Shaula of the Bonecrown coven, Corvina's predecessor, realized there were more females than males. She got a secret army together and attacked. In one night, she slaughtered eighty percent of the warlock population. All because they weren't expecting such a betrayal. They weren't prepared."

"Wait ... what about Bagatha? The Queen of All Witches?"

"She had already passed on her powers to the Witch Queens and went into hiding," he explained. "It was shortly after. I guess Shaula had always been power hungry, and she suddenly saw an opportunity."

"What happened to the other twenty percent of the warlocks?"

"I rallied them to fight back," he said, his voice sorrowful. "We did, but the witches outnumbered us twelve to one. Many of us lost our lives fighting for justice. Until I realized we wouldn't win that way and ordered the warlocks to flee. We spent a long while in hiding." He jerked his chin to the manor's direction. "We built this place in secret, regained our strength, tried to rebuild our army ... and started to fight back. We haven't been hiding for many years, but the witches still outnumber us and most of them still see us as aberrations that should be killed on sight."

That was so different from what Queen Corvina had told us. Why would she lie? "What now? Are you still fighting with them?"

"When they threaten us, yes." He nodded. "The Bonecrown witches are always threatening us."

It didn't make sense. Why would Queen Corvina send me here, directly to my father, if he was her enemy? "I should talk to Thea. I'm sure that she can think of something and come up with a peace treaty. Then, witches and warlocks can live in peace."

Soren's lips stretched in a sad smile. "I like that you're young and optimistic. It means your soul hasn't been tainted by betrayals and evil."

I frowned. "What do you mean?"

"Unfortunately, my son, there will never be peace among witches and warlocks." He stared at me with his dark eyes, fervor shining from them. "The only way for peace to reign is if I defeat the witches and enforce peace."

"W-what?"

"Stay here, my son. Stay with me. Join me, become my right arm in the war to come. Together, we'll be unstoppable. We'll take over the witch covens and make them bow to us." His voice rose and the glint in his eyes gained a crazed hue. "They've had it good for too long, slaughtering thousands of warlocks over the years and pushing us back." He shot to his feet. "No more! It's our turn now. We can start a new era!"

Slowly, I stood and took a step back from this crazy man. "But ... that's wrong. What Thea and Drake advocate is all races living in peace, including warlocks and witches."

"We'll live in peace, after we put the witches in their places."

I shook my head. "No. That isn't right."

"Well, it'll depend if the other races also submit to us," he went on, only half-listening to me. "The details don't matter. What matters is that you join me, and we become the most powerful warlocks the world has ever seen."

I took another step back. "Soren ..." Would it help if I called him father? "Father ... what you're doing is wrong."

"Just think about it." He rushed to me and came to a sudden halt in front of me. "With the command of the warlocks, you can save Luana's pack from Isalia's clutches."

I blinked at him. "How do you know that?"

"You think I would let a werewolf into my coven and not know anything about her?" He shook his head, as if he was disappointed in me. "I also know you're in love with her, and you would do anything for her."

In love with her.

Yes, I was. It was a shame it took a deranged man to say it out loud for me to recognize it. But it was true, I loved Luana.

Although, Luana wouldn't want this. She would never forgive me if I joined this mad man to save her pack. She would rather die with them all.

And I would rather die than join the warlock standing in front of me.

I let out a long sigh. So much disappointment. I had come here with such high hopes and eagerness, only to find out my father was evil. Now, he just needed to confess all he told me was a lie, and Queen Corvina told me the truth.

Then what about the prophecy? Was that true too? I knew if I asked, he wouldn't answer, and if he did, I wouldn't know if he was lying again.

"This isn't right." I took a step back. "I thank you for your hospitality, but my friends and I are leaving."

I spun around, ready to run back to the manor.

Dark shadows surrounded me, closing me in darkness. Soren stepped into the darkness with me.

"You're not going anywhere."

23

LUANA

I PACED THE ROOM, GROWING STEADILY AGITATED.

"You'll wear a hole in the floor," Wyatt said.

I made a rude gestured to him and Farrah chuckled.

I had been in Wyatt's room since Virion had come to take Keeran to see his father, almost an hour ago. I hadn't meant to, but with my hearing, I had listened to everything. Even the way Keeran's heart spiked at certain moments when he was alone, as if he remembered something.

Like the way he had kissed me last night.

A heat wave rushed through my body, and I did my best to conceal any changes from Wyatt. With his senses, he would be able to tell something was different in no time.

Like my desperate lust for Keeran, and my desperate need to know where he was and what exactly he was doing.

The fact that I had found out he was my mate didn't influence any of my feelings. Nope. No way. I had always cared for him.

But not like this.

By the moon …

If there wasn't this feeling in my gut telling something bad was about to happen, my nerves wouldn't be so spooked, and I wouldn't be pacing as if I could find an answer after wearing down the floor.

"Okay, I can't take this anymore." I marched to the door.

"Where are you going?" Wyatt asked.

"I'm going to find Keeran," I told him. Like me, he and Farrah didn't trust the warlocks and wanted to leave. "You two stay here until I come back. Got it?"

Wyatt nodded. "Yes, ma'am."

I rolled my eyes at him. I hated when he called me that.

I heard his whisper to Farrah as I closed the room's door. "I think she likes him."

"And I'm sure he likes her," Farrah whispered back.

If only it were that simple.

Out in the corridor, I sniffed the air, trying to get a hold of Keeran's scent and follow him, but there must be something in the air or some kind of spell, because I couldn't make out any scents.

Now, I was even more wary of these damn warlocks.

I made my way to the stairs and spied down, focusing on my hearing. No one. Not even a creak. What the hell was happening here?

On high alert, I went down the stairs.

I paused at the second-floor landing.

Something barreled into me, pushing hard against my stomach, taking my breath away.

Holy shit.

I was thrown several feet back. My head spun. I blinked, trying to get a hold of my bearings, but the force struck again, pushing me back another several feet. I rolled past a doorframe.

"What—?" I croaked, but my words died as another force wrapped around my wrists, neck, and chest and pulled me up. Off the ground. I shook my head once, trying to clear my vision. Slowly, they came into focus.

Warlocks. Several of them.

Standing in front of the bunch, Virion had his hand up. He was the one holding me up here.

"Why did you come?" he asked, his voice loud and rough. I jerked against the hold. The pressure around my neck lessened a little and I sucked in a sharp breath. "Answer me!" Virion boomed.

"I don't owe you any answers," I spat. Who did he think I was? Even if coming here to check out Soren was a simple and true enough answer, I wouldn't tell him that now, not after he pushed me around like a big sack of potato.

"You came to kill Soren," Virion said. Not a question. "I won't let it happen. Even if I have to kill all of you myself." The magic tightened around my throat again, and I gasped for air. "Starting with you."

For a brief second, desperation took hold of me. Then, I closed my eyes and focused. I calmed down, enough to call on my wolf and shift. But nothing happened. My wolf clawed from the inside out, but I couldn't shift. This damn magic holding me didn't let me shift.

If I didn't shift, I wouldn't have a chance of fighting against these warlocks.

Of escaping.

I was as good as dead.

The desperation hit me hard. Not only because I was

going to die, but Keeran, Wyatt, and Farrah probably would too.

I couldn't let that happen.

A howl tore from my throat. My wolf expanded inside me, begging for release. My howl became a scream as pain spread through my muscles, my veins, my pores.

Everything hurt.

I went limp, held up only by magic, magic that squeezed me tighter and tighter.

"Let her go!" someone shouted.

I forced my head up and stared as more warlocks came into the room and threw black bolts at the others. A fight began.

Virion was hit in the chest.

I fell on the ground hard, my knees jarring on the impact with the hard floor.

I scooted back, trying to understand what was going on. All I saw was a bunch of warlocks dressed in black fighting each other. If there were sides, I couldn't distinguish any. Magic pellets ricocheted from the spells, and I scooted back more, avoiding them.

This was my chance. I had to shift and get Keeran, Wyatt, and Farrah and *run*. We couldn't stay in this crazy, forsaken place a second longer.

I started to shift when one warlock ran at me. "Wait, don't. We're on your side."

That gave me pause, but I was too wary to trust anyone right now. "How do I know you're telling the truth?"

A grunt came from behind him. He turned around, just as a bloodied Virion came for him, his hand raised, calling for his magic. The warlock in front of me was faster. He conjured a blade of magic and threw it at Virion. The blade pierced

Virion's chest, right into his heart. Virion's eyes widened, his steps faltered. Then the blade exploded, and blood flew everything.

Virion's mangled body hit the floor with a sickening wet thump.

My stomach turned.

Around us, the fighting faded as the young warlock's group won.

He turned to me. "I'm Zell, and I would like to help you take Soren down."

"I DON'T WANT TO FIGHT YOU."

A wicked grin cut through my father's face. "I don't think you have a choice, son. You either fight me or die right now. It's your choice." He shrugged. "Not that fighting me will change the outcome. You'll die anyway."

He threw a black ray at me.

I jumped to the side and ran into the darkness. He was too strong for me to fight him like that. If I were ever to take him down, I would need help. I kept my hands in front of me as I ran through the dark orchard. In the span of ten seconds, I bumped into four trees, but finally I seemed to have broken through past the orchard. However, darkness still enveloped the garden and I was lost to which direction to go.

As if a huge fan had been turned on, the darkness pushed out, clearing the space around me, but keeping tall walls several feet away, like a dome made of pure smoke.

"You have nowhere to run, Keeran." My father stepped through the smoke. "This is your last chance. Join me or die."

A rush of anger coursed through me. How could I have been so stupid and think he was a good guy? He wasn't. He would never be.

Taking advantage of the anger running through my veins, I called on my magic. I might not be able to kill him, but I would fight him until I found an opening to run. I still had to factor in finding Luana, Wyatt, and Farrah into my timing.

This would suck.

Soren threw several arrow-like bolts at me. I waved my hand in front of me, creating a shield. The arrows slammed into the shield, crumbling upon contact, but the shield flickered with each one, until it broke.

One last arrow flew at me, and I twisted before it could pierce my heart. It grazed my shoulder, ripping my shirt and scratching my skin.

I hissed.

Enraged, I threw a large bolt of red energy at Soren.

Soren raised his hand and stopped the bolt halfway. Laughing, he clenched his fist and the bolt imploded, fading away as if it had never existed.

Despair clutched my gut as I realized that I could try, I could pretend, but I was no match for him.

I braced myself for his next round of spells, but the duel seemed to stop as warlocks appeared at the edge of the shadow dome.

Soren's warlocks. They were here to see me fail.

To see me die.

Another boost to my self-doubt. My magic was unstable when I called for it.

As I predicted, Soren sent a bolt at me. Then another. And another.

I dodged them all, jogging around the dome as if I was in

a dodgeball game. Soren was playing with me, making fun of me, exhausting while he laughed in my face.

In no time, I would be crawling like a half-dead cockroach.

I couldn't run forever.

Planting my feet firmly on the ground, I inhaled deeply and channeled my power. I thought of my terrible past; of Thea and Drake, who saved me and gave purpose; of Luana, who I cared about more than anything else in this world; of my mother, who was hiding, afraid of the horrible man standing in front of me; of the prophecy and what it meant for me, for all of us; and of him, my father, an evil warlock, who didn't deserve the power he had.

I opened my hands and a big red bolt appeared, floating between my palms. A shout burst from my throat as I let the bolt go, throwing it at Soren.

I wasn't surprised when he took the bolt, but I had expected him to make it disappear again, not take control of it. A wicked grin curled his lips as he hurled the bolt at me.

I didn't have time to run. The bolt exploded against my chest, pushing me back several feet. I fell hard on the grass, the air flying from my lungs. Pain spread through my chest and arms.

Groaning, I pushed up on my elbows.

Soren stalked over.

Shit. I was going to die.

A shadow jumped from the edge of the dome. My breath caught.

Luana!

In her wolf form, she jumped right on top of Soren, pushing him down. Surprised, he didn't have time to react as Luana closed her jaw around his shoulder.

Soren screamed before lashing out with his magic and flinging Luana aside as if she was a fly.

Following Luana's attack, a group of warlocks stepped into the dome and a battle began—warlocks against warlocks.

I gasped as realization hit me. There were two groups. One with Soren, and another with Luana.

With me.

Groaning, I pushed up. A wave of dizziness rushed through me, and I gritted my teeth, forcing it down.

A few feet from me, Luana advanced on Soren. I felt the crackle in the air, the energy being sucked away, as Soren channeled his power. He was going to send a hit to Luana, and it was going to be deadly.

I simply threw my hands out and let my magic fly. A red ray hit Soren's hands and he lost his grip on his magic. With Luana by my side, I knew we could do it; I knew we could defeat this monster.

Luana let out a yelp, and I knew what she meant.

She ran to the side, feigning attacks toward Soren. Distracting him.

With Luana in mind, I created a bigger bolt, a more powerful bolt. Luana was ready. She shifted toward me again, making Soren turn. His eyes on her, he didn't even notice he was unguarded.

I threw the bolt.

It exploded against his chest.

Soren fell and Luana jumped on him. She pressed her paws against Soren's chest, keeping him in place. To emphasize she was serious about mauling him, she snapped her sharp teeth at him. I approached them, looming over my father, and channeled my power.

This was it. This was when I killed the son of a bitch and ended his reign of darkness.

Soren put his hand over his heart. "Would you kill your father?"

The way he said it, the sweetly disappointed tone of his voice, the hurt in his eyes ... I hesitated. I shouldn't have, but I hesitated. After all, the bastard was my father.

But he was evil.

Someone had to take him out.

I could be that someone.

I called a red bolt to my hands—

Soren's magic exploded from him, sending Luana and me back. Groaning as the pain spread my body, I rolled to my side and gasped.

Soren was gone.

I pushed to my knees and looked around. The shadow dome dissipated into smoke rising to the sky and the brightness of the sun hurt my eyes for a moment.

And Soren was gone.

Around me, the battle winded down. Some warlocks ran —Soren's men who didn't want to face their end. Bodies of warlocks littered the garden, their blood tainting the grass.

Still in wolf form, Luana approached me. She yelped, and somehow, I knew what she was asking.

"Yes, I'm ... fine. I think. How about you?"

She nodded her head once.

Then, a young warlock stepped closer to us. I shot to my feet and channeled my magic.

The warlock raised his hands to attack.

"He's on our side," Luana said. I glanced to the side, and she was crouched in the grass, having shifted.

I took off my shirt and placed it over her shoulders. "What do you mean?"

She slipped her arms through the sleeves and pulled the shirt tight around herself as she stood beside me. "This is Zell. He saved me from Virion earlier. He said he wanted to take Soren down."

Wait. Virion had attacked Luana. "What about Wyatt and Farrah?"

Luana frowned. "Safe in their rooms, I hope."

I turned to Zell. "What happened? Why are you on our side?"

"Soren is a tyrant," he said. The remaining warlocks gathered behind him, all listening closely. "We put on a show for when you arrived yesterday, but that was all it was. A show. We've been treated unfairly and sent to the depths of the Earth to find Acalla and you. And when we came back without you, he tortured us. The humans you've seen around the castle? They are slaves. Soren put an illusion spell on them so you wouldn't see how bad they really look. Not to mention the witches. There are a dozen or so witches locked in our dungeons. They are used for breeding."

I shook my head.

Believing Soren was evil was one thing. Finding out all the bad things he had done? It was sickening.

"But why?" I muttered.

"The prophecy is true," Zell said, his gray eyes serious. "The prophecy says you're the only one with enough power to stop him. Since you refused to stand by him, he now wants to kill you and steal your power. More powerful than ever, he would march on the Bonecrown witches to kill them all and take over their lands. But he wouldn't stop there. He would take his army coven by coven, until all the witches were gone."

He was mad. Utterly mad. "But he's not dead. I didn't defeat him. He ran." Which meant, this wasn't done. He would come back for me.

"That's why we urge you to stay here," Zell said. "Become the Warlock Lord and guide us into a better future."

I sucked in a sharp breath. I glanced at Luana. She was looking at her feet. "But ... I'm not strong enough."

"You are," Zell said. "We can all feel the power emanating from you." The other warlocks nodded. "It's much stronger than Soren's. You just need to learn how to access it and use it. We can help you." He paused. "And when Soren comes back, you'll be ready to finish him once and for all."

Everything was happening too fast. Until a couple of hours ago, I thought I had a chance of putting my family back together and living in peace. Then, my father had attacked me. Now, I learned he was out to steal my power and kill me, before he marched on to the witches to eliminate them all.

And now they wanted me to claim the status of Warlock Lord?

"I don't know ..."

"We've lived in fear for far too many years," Zell said, a plea to his voice. "You're our only hope, Keeran. Please."

My gut twisted.

When he put it like that ...

I looked at Luana again. She still wouldn't meet my eyes.

First, I had rejected her. Last night, she had rejected me. We were on our own again, each of us wanting to belong. She had her pack to go back to and claim. And I had the warlocks. Things looked bad, but if I invoked what I had learned from

Thea and Drake, I believed I could make a better coven. Or I could at least try.

Pride filled my chest, along with purpose.

Finally, I had found where I belonged.

I inhaled deeply. "I'll do it."

MY HEART WILTED WITH EACH PASSING MINUTE.

Right after Keeran accepted becoming the Warlock Lord of the Dark Witch Manor, we jumped into action. We cleaned up the garden, disposed of the bodies, healed the injured from the battle, treated the human slaves who were badly hurt and freed them, and went after the witches locked in the dungeons. Most were Bonecrown witches, but there were a couple from Wildthorn and even one from the Silverblood coven. Like the ex-slaves, we treated their wounds, fed them, then provided them with a couple of bedrooms so they could shower and put on decent clothes. Then, we let them go.

There was still a lot of work to do, a lot of things to figure out, but that was the warlocks' problem, not mine.

My time here had ended.

Early the next morning, I was in my bedroom, packing a small bag with a change of clothes and other necessities when Keeran walked in. I quickly pushed the crystalized rose to the bottom of the bag. He looked exhausted, but happy. As if he had found his calling.

He skidded to a stop when he saw the open duffel bag over the bed. "What are you doing?"

"What does it look like?" I flinched over my harsh words, but what did he expect me to say? He knew what this meant.

He took deliberate steps toward me. "But ... why?"

I shrugged. It was still hard looking at him, because even without looking at him, I could feel the intense pull of the mating call. When I looked at him, it was too hard to fight it. "You've found your place. I should get back to mine."

"But ..." He ran a hand through his messy hair, messing it up some more. "Stay just a little longer. It's a little chaotic right now, and I need to set this boat straight before I let it sail, but I would love your help."

"There are plenty of warlocks ready to help you. They know this place much better than I ever will."

"I just ... I want you to stay."

My heart wilted. "That's not up for discussion."

"Then just stay so I can get my feet under me, and in a couple of days, I can repay the favor. I can help you. I now can ask all the warlocks to help us. Together, we can take down Isalia."

I shook my head. "I appreciate the offer, but you know I have to take her down alone, without cheating, to be a worthy alpha."

"But she won't play fair again! The warlocks and I can at least hold the rest of her supporters back while you fight her, like we talked about."

That was the best plan we had come up with so far, but right now, I was hurting too much. I needed distance from him and this place.

"I ... I just need to go."

He reached for me. "Luana ..."

I took a step back, getting out of reach. "If you really want to help me, then let me go. I promise I won't engage Isalia in any way, but I need to go. I'll find her, I'll assess the situation, her army, and I'll send word to you. Then, you come with your warlocks and help me take her out." Deep inside, I knew I wouldn't do that. I would find my own way to defeat her, but right now, I would say anything so he wouldn't make this harder than it already was.

His brows slammed down. "You should stay too—"

"I need to go," I cut him off. "Isalia found me in the middle of a ghost town. She could be anywhere right now." Hopefully, she would be back at the pack. It would be easier to attack her in a place I knew well. "The faster I find her, the less my pack will suffer."

Finally, Keeran nodded. "I understand. I don't like it. But I understand."

I shoved the last of my things in the bag, zipped it up, and slung it over my shoulder. Portraying what I hoped was a calm and determined expression, I turned to Keeran. "Congratulations on becoming Warlock Lord."

He shrugged. "As if I deserved it."

"I know you'll be a great leader, like Drake and Thea. You'll make them proud." He would make me proud. A painful pang cut through my heart. "Take care, Keeran."

His heart sped up, and he took a slow inhale to try and slow it down. He knew I could hear it. "You promise you'll wait for me. Just call me and I'll be there."

I nodded, because I couldn't lie again, not out loud. "Thank you."

I sidestepped him and marched toward the door.

"Luana," he called, my name a soft whisper in his lips.

Holding my breath, I spied over my shoulder. "Yes?"

He stared at me, his dark eyes troubled. "Take care."

"You too."

I took a step forward. Then another. Then another.

When I was finally out in the corridor, I let out a long breath as my chest ripped open with pain and longing. I was leaving. I was leaving my mate behind.

I was sure he didn't love me now, but if we surrendered to the mating call, I knew it was a possibility. But since I was leaving, I knew he would never be able to love another—because no one else was meant to be his.

For that, I felt like an even bigger bitch.

Wyatt appeared by my side, a knot between his brows. "Let's go," he said in a low voice. The young wolf might not feel the mating call, but he sure knew about my feelings for Keeran, even if only by the involuntary changes in my body whenever he was near me.

And now, as I walked away from him.

To make matters worse, I knew Wyatt wasn't happy about leaving. I had told him to stay, but he said he was a part of the pack too and he would help me get it back, no matter what.

We walked through the busy castle practically unseen as the warlocks rushed around, putting everything in order and helping the recently freed humans and witches.

The sun was high and warm outside, and I had to close my eyes for a second to get used to its brightness. In silence, we followed the path skirting the mountain. I didn't like being this quiet. It gave too much room in my mind for thoughts that weren't welcome.

Instead, I thought of my strategy. Wyatt and I would avoid Bonecrown witch territory as we went down the mountain.

We would go east to the nearest road, follow that road until we found a gas station, a rest stop, or a small town, and steal a car. Then, we would drive nonstop back to our side of the state, where the pack was.

This time, we wouldn't be caught by Isalia, because we wouldn't stop, we wouldn't relax. Earlier, Wyatt had asked me, "What if we get back to the pack and Isalia isn't there?"

I had thought about that too. Didn't it seem like she was following us? Following me? She had found us in the middle of nowhere and challenged me again. If she wasn't with the pack, then it meant she was following me—and this way, she would follow me right back to the pack.

And that was where I was going to kill her.

We crossed the invisible line marking the end of the Dark Witch Manor territory and Wyatt grunted.

I glanced at him. "Are you okay?"

"Yeah, it's just ..." he gasped. "Luana!"

A boom exploded in my skull and my vision darkened. Pain rippled through my head, down my neck, and my body became numb. I blinked, fighting the pain and the dizziness taking over me, but I felt the darkness enveloping me.

I fell to the ground.

A second later, Wyatt dropped beside me.

"Wy—" I tried calling him, but the words got stuck in my throat.

I saw a pair of feet appear between us, but as the person crouched and got closer, the world became dark.

And I blacked out.

THANK YOU

THANK YOU FOR READING *THE WARLOCK LORD*!

Reviews are very important for authors. If you liked my book, please consider leaving a review on amazon and/or on goodreads, please!

You can pre-order book 2 now:

The Wolf Consort

Don't forget to sign up for my Newsletter to find out about new releases, cover reveals, giveaways, and more!

If you want to see exclusive teasers, help me decide on covers, read excerpts, talk about books, etc, join my reader group on Facebook: Juliana's Club!

ABOUT THE AUTHOR

While USA Today Bestselling Author Juliana Haygert dreams of being Wonder Woman, Buffy, or a blood elf shadow priest, she settles for the less exciting—but equally gratifying—life as a wife, a mother, and an author. Thousands of miles away from her former home in Brazil, she now resides in North Carolina and spends her days writing about kick-ass heroines and the heroes who drive them crazy.

Subscribe to her mailing list to receive emails of announcement, events, and other fun stuff related to her writing and her books: www.bit.ly/JuHNL

For more information:
www.julianahaygert.com

f facebook.com/julianahaygert

🐦 twitter.com/juliana_haygert

📷 instagram.com/juliana.haygert

ALSO BY JULIANA HAYGERT

www.julianahaygert.com/books/

Free

Into the Darkest Fire

Tested

Secret Santa

Rite World: Rite of the Vampire

The Vampire Heir (Book 1)

The Witch Queen (Book 2)

The Immortal Vow (Book 3)

Rite World: Rite of the Warlock

The Warlock Lord (Book 1)

The Wolf Consort (Book 2)

The Crystal Rose (Book 3)

The Everlast Series

Destiny Gift (Book 1)

Soul Oath (Book 2)

Cup of Life (Book 3)

Everlasting Circle (Book 4)

The Fire Heart Chronicles

Heart Seeker (Book 1)

Flame Caster (Book 2)

Sorrow Bringer (Book 3)

Earth Shaker (Novella)

Soul Wanderer (Book 4)

Fate Summoner (Book 5)

War Maiden (Book 6)

Willow Harbor Series

Hunter's Revenge (Book 3)

Siren's Song (Book 5)

The Breaking Series

Breaking Free (Book 1)

Breaking Away (Book 2)

Breaking Through (Book 3)

Standalones

Playing Pretend

Captured Love

Dazzle Me

Printed in Great Britain
by Amazon

45275389R00137